Dustin

MCCULLOUGH'S JAMBOREE BOOK 3

KATHI S. BARTON

World Castle Publishing, LLC
Pensacola, Florida
Copyright © Kathi S. Barton 2017
Paperback ISBN: 9781629897776
eBook ISBN: 9781629897783
First Edition World Castle Publishing, LLC, August 21, 2017
http://www.worldcastlepublishing.com

Licensing Notes

Cover: Karen Fuller
Editor: Maxine Bringenberg

Chapter 1

Pacing the long hallway didn't make things go any faster, but he had to do something or he was going to hit someone. Dustin wasn't much of an idle person...none of his brothers were. But this waiting stuff, it was for the birds. As he started to move down the other hallway for a change of scenery, he paused when he saw the man.

There wasn't anything strange about him, not if you discounted the fact that he was poorly dressed and his shirt was full of holes. He seemed to be clean...he didn't smell dirty or have sweat on him. But when another man came out of one of the curtained off rooms — an orderly, Dustin supposed — he moved closer to hear what was being said. The elderly man didn't strike him as being someone that he should be wary of, but Dustin was bored and interested in different things, he told himself. Besides, Dustin's new employee was back there, and he didn't want him hurt if this went badly.

"Mac here? I got me some pains, and I was told to come on back here if it didn't get better." The orderly nodded and said that Mac had come in about an hour ago. "Do you think that I can have a few minutes? I've got me a powerful pain in my foot, and I was told to come in if it didn't get any better."

"Yes, but you'll need to sign in." The man nodded, but he didn't move. "I can call Mac, but you have to sign in before I will. There are rules, Rubin, and you know that. I'll page her, but you have to sign in for us."

"Yes, I know that, but I don't know how to read. I told you that the last time I was here. Can you find me someone to help an old man out?" The man that had been talking to Rubin moved back behind the curtained area, leaving Rubin all alone. "Damn it, boy, I told you I was hurting. Nobody wants to come and help an old man out anymore. What's this here world coming to when you can't even—?"

"Can I help you?" Rubin turned to look at him and Dustin smiled at him. "I can assist you with the paperwork if that'll help you. My employee is getting his hand stitched up and should be a little while longer. I don't mind helping you out if you need it."

"They are mean to me here. I don't mean that they should put out a red carpet or nothing, but they could at least let a man have some dignity. Why do I have to sign in when they all know who I am and why I'm here?" Dustin said that he was sorry about that. "Your friend, he have insurance? They treat you differently when you don't have any. Sort of stick you in a room for hours on end and forget about you."

"I don't think that's true, but who knows? Yes, he has some through my company." Rubin nodded, but looked back at the man who had disappeared. "I don't mind helping you, sir. If you just tell me what has to be done we'll get you signed in so you can go see the doctor."

"I have to fill out one of them papers that tells them my name and such. I can write my name good, but not read a lick of words. Letters were never my strong suit." Dustin followed him, pushing his wheelchair to the desk for him, where a nice nurse gave him what Rubin needed. Sitting down, Dustin started asking him the questions that were on the form.

"Rubin Davis."

His age surprised him. Dustin would have thought him much younger than his seventy-four years. "Address and phone number?"

"I live on the streets. I have a post office box number that they say won't work, but that's all I got. Mac set that up for me." Dustin nodded and put his own address down. "What are you writing there?"

"My address and phone number. I'm going to see about getting you a cell phone, all right?" Rubin asked him why he'd do something like that. "I don't know. I'm sort of bored and I need to do something. Helping you will get me in good with my mom. She's a little upset with me right now."

"You only get yourself one mom, and you'd better take care not to upset her. She mean to you or just stern?" He told him that she was never mean, but she could peel rubber off a tire when she was upset. "Yeah, my mom was like that too. Loved her to pieces, but I was terrified of her too. Schooling wasn't helping much, and I was getting on her last frayed nerve. Then one day, I got myself in a fix that even she couldn't help me with. Judge told me, 'Join up or jail.' That's why I joined up in the service when I did. Momma could use the money, so that's what I did."

"I'm afraid of my mom too. All us boys are." Rubin asked him how many there were of them. "I have five brothers and two sisters-in-law. I'm afraid of them as well. And in awe. They're very strong women. One of them was in the Army as well."

"All women are strong, but they don't usually know it. Some of them have to have a good man bring it out of them. You got yourself a woman?" He told him just his mom. "Well, that won't keep you warm at night, but that's a good answer."

After finishing the paperwork, Dustin turned it in and waited with him. The nurse that had taken Randy back told him that he'd be a bit longer. They were making sure there wasn't anything in the cut before they stitched it up. The kid had already cost him a lot of time, and now he was going to have to wait longer. Not that he didn't enjoy sitting with Rubin, but Randy had been a pain in their sides since his first day. He was the most stubborn, pigheaded person he'd ever hired. And now he was going to have to let him go.

He'd told him five times not to use the drill so close to his hand. It was like the kid had a death wish when it came to electrical equipment. The first day he'd been on the job, three days ago, he'd cut his hand on the electric tile cutter, and it hadn't been on or even plugged in. The second day, yesterday, he'd cut his foot on the table saw. Dustin was still trying to figure out how the hell he'd done that. Fucking around was all he could think of. Now today he'd rammed the drill through the middle of his palm and tore it up badly.

"You don't have to wait here with me." He told Rubin that he wanted to. "Well, I thank you, son. Not many people would want to be around an old man like me. I been talking to Mac, my doctor, since I moved here about five months ago. Not into practicing medicine much anymore. She got hurt one night working ER and never been the same. Hell of a surgeon, though. Been watching over me and my diabetes. I've got it bad, and the meds I take, they ain't cheap for me. But I got me this card that helps me out a lot."

"My brother is a doctor. Boyd McCullough. He has a nice practice not far from here, but he was busy today and so I had to bring Randy here." They talked about this and that, and after about an hour, a man came out to talk to Rubin. Not the one that had been rude to him earlier.

"Mr. Davis, I've heard from Mac. I was told to set you up in one of the rooms down here, and that as soon as possible, you'll be seen. All right?" Rubin said that was just fine. "Also, I'm to ask you if you've been taking your medications."

"Yes. I was told if I didn't, I'd get my ass handed to me." The nurse said that was good and stood up. Rubin turned to Dustin. "You gonna come with me? I'd surely like the company if you don't mind."

"No, I don't mind. Let me check on Randy and I'll be right with you." Rubin said he'd be right down the hall. Dustin made his way to the cubicle Randy was in.

"You can go on home, Dustin. My wife is coming to get me. And she's none too happy with me." Dustin wanted to point out he wasn't either, but only nodded. "I should have listened to you about that drill. I'm very sorry about all this."

"Just take some time off and get healed. But I can't have you doing things your own way when you think you know it all." Randy nodded. "I'll talk to my dad, and we'll see what we can do about this in the future."

"I understand." Dustin wasn't sure he did, and when he told him he'd see him next week, he knew it. "I can't lose my job, Dustin. I need it."

"We'll talk." As he made his way back to see Rubin, he

reached out to his dad to tell him what was going on. *I'm not going to be coming back just yet. I'm sitting with an elderly gentleman who asked me to stay with him. I'll be there soon.*

Take your time. We're doing much better since that kid is gone. My goodness gracious, Dustin, the kid was lucky that he only messed up his hand and didn't take his fool head off. Dustin agreed with him and told his dad they'd have to fire him. *Yes, we'll do that. Shame too. But it's dangerous when you don't listen to someone that knows better.*

He found Rubin easily enough, and sat in the little room's only chair. He'd been in the ER for over three hours now, and figured that since his day was shot, he might as well sit with this man Besides, he really enjoyed his company. As they talked about nothing again, such as what Dustin did for a living, Rubin told him what he'd done when he was a younger man.

"Trouble mostly when I was a youngster. Then the Army, as I said. All the way. I didn't know that I had it so good until I was out. Of course, there are people that spend more time in there than they should. Like my Mac. Never seen a person that could go between the two worlds, civilian and Army, like that one." He told Rubin about Lauren. "Lauren Burcher? You know her?"

"Yes, she's my sister-in-law." Rubin stared at him, then burst out laughing. It made him smile to see someone enjoy a bit of information as much as Rubin seemed to have. "She and my brother, Colin, are parents now. They have two sets of twins. Two girls and two boys. I think she was under the impression that she was going to be able to whip them into shape the first day. It's been a couple months, and I don't think her plan is working."

"She's a hoot, I tell you. I only met her the one time....
It was a few years ago. When she came to tell me about my
grandboy." Dustin knew then that Rubin's grandson had
fought with her. "I just realized something too. You're Hawk's
brother, aren't you?"

"Yes. Hawkins is one of my brothers." Dustin looked
around the room then back at Rubin before he spoke again.
"Something wrong with that?"

"No. But I'm thinking you don't have any idea who Mac
is, do you?" Dustin said that he didn't know him. "Mac ain't
no male, son. She's a she. And her and Hawk, they don't get
on very well."

He started to ask him what that meant, but the curtain
opened and he was sure he was staring at the infamous Mac.
She came in, sat on the side of the bed, and ignored him
over Rubin. Dustin reached out to Lauren, never sure where
Hawkins was, and asked about a doctor or surgeon named
Mac.

Mackenzie Gibson? She's there at the hospital with you? He
told her what was going on. *Holy Christ, Dustin. You're in for a
shitstorm if she figures out who you are.*

I think she knows. I filled out the paperwork for my friend here.
She told him to leave, now. *What's going on?*

*I'll tell you about it, what I can, when you get here. Leave now,
before she shows you what a nice little temper she has.* He stood
up and Mac told him to sit. He told Lauren. *I'll remember you
well,* was all she said before she started laughing and closed
the connection.

Dustin wasn't sure what to do, and sat there with his
mouth shut. Fuck this shit; he didn't need it, and when he
stood again she did as well. Dustin swallowed three times

before he could speak. Christ, she was gorgeous. Sitting down again, she did as well. But he was sure that they sat for different reasons. He did because she made him weak in the knees.

~~~

Ignoring the man, she sat back down. Looking at Rubin, she asked him what was going on with him that brought him in today. She was his friend first and his doctor second. Right now, she had to wear the latter hat to try and stem the fear she had of the man by the bed.

"Got me some toe issues. You said that I had to keep it clean and all, but I'm not sure I did such a good job this time." Mac stood up and started unlacing Rubin's boot. "But I've been taking my medications like you told me, and I've been eating like I should. Well, when I could get me a meal, that is. No reason for my foot to be a bothering me like it is."

Mac could smell it even as she slipped his boot off. It was infected. And there was blood on his sock. She knew even before she saw the foot that he was going to lose it. Gangrene had set in. Glancing at the man who was holding onto Rubin's hand, she tried to decide how to tell him.

"You're gonna take it off, ain't you?" She nodded at Rubin. "I been really careful and all, I promise you. I don't want to be losing my foot, Doc. I know that I got me another one, but this one here, it comes in handy when I'm walking around and dancing a jig or two with a pretty woman like yourself. If you can fix me up, I'm sure that I can make it work out for me."

"I'm sorry, Rubin, I truly am. Sometimes no matter what you do, this is the way it goes, and I hate to do it as much as you hate it. But if I leave it, you'll die. I told you when I saw you last time that this might happen." Mac wanted to go home, be anywhere but there. The man with her friend was a McCullough, and there was no denying it even if she'd not read his name on the chart. There couldn't have been two men that looked more alike than these two. And having to deliver bad news on top of that was almost too much to bear. "When was the last time you ate anything?"

In her mind, she was trying to calculate the times. Surgery on his foot would be hard on the elderly man…her too if she was honest. And the man, Dustin McCullough, was too distracting. She wondered what his connection to Rubin was, but wasn't going to ask. She wasn't even sure why she'd told him to sit down. Mac should have let him go home or whatever.

Going to the front desk, she started making plans for the surgery. Rubin had nothing—less than nothing—so she also signed off on the paperwork to have his bills sent to her home. Not that there would be that much after this, but she didn't want him burdened.

Just as she was hanging up the phone, Lauren Burcher came into the emergency room like she owned the place. Mac had been so impressed with the other woman when she'd worked with her all those years ago. That was before she had turned her temper and her connections on her. It had taken Mac less time to get out of the service than it had for her to get in. Thanks, in part, to Lauren Burcher. When she came up to her, smiling that smile that never boded well for anyone, Mac waited.

"Mac." Mac nodded, but didn't speak. She was more concerned with where Hawkins was. "He's out of the country if it's Hawk that you're looking for. He still goes out and brings the injured or dying home. What are you doing here?"

"I work here off and on. Not that I have to justify myself to you." Lauren smiled. "What the fuck are you doing here? Are you going to get me fired again? Or perhaps you'd like to have my license revoked? At this point, I don't care if you do either. But know this is my turf, and I have a bit more pull than you do." At least she hoped she did. With Lauren, it was difficult to tell where she had loyal friends.

"Fired? No, I never did that to you. I've come to rescue Dustin. Have you chewed him up and spit him out like you did Hawkins when he asked you for a favor?" She wanted to slap the other woman, but was afraid she'd kill her. There was never an in-between with Lauren. It was always all go or she'd ignore the situation. And she'd never done the latter with Mac. "Have you told him?"

"Told him what?" Lauren snorted. "Look, I have work to do. If you have nothing productive to say to me, then I'd like for you to take Dustin home and leave me to my work."

"That's too fucking bad. He's here of his own accord, with a friend. Do you have any of those? And I'm talking about the fact that you ignored a request, a very nice one, from his brother. That you left a woman to suffer in the worst sort of way." It was right there, on the tip of her tongue, to tell Lauren to fuck off, she'd not done a damned thing, but there were things going on back then, and now, that she had no control over. "I'm assuming that you're denying that still."

"I have work to do, Lauren. If there is nothing more, I'm going to leave you here." She turned away, then looked back. "For all this hotshot shit kicker that everyone thinks you are, you're about the laziest woman I've ever met when it comes to getting all your facts in a row, aren't you? Perhaps, just maybe, you should have done your research a little better before assuming the worst about me and what I was doing. I would have before I did what you did to me."

She left her standing there. Mac had an operating room to prep and forms to fill out, and standing around debating what sort of person she was to a pigheaded woman wasn't going to get them done. However, just as she got off the elevator on the surgical floor, she turned left instead of right to go into her office. Closing and locking the door behind her, she stood against the door and let the tears fall.

It hadn't been that long ago, but to her it seemed a lifetime of horror. Every time she closed her eyes it would haunt her. Every time she had to go into the emergency room, she'd think of the man that had lain there, his gut hanging out, his arm barely hanging onto his hand by a bit of skin and muscle. And Hawk standing there, his rifle pointed at her, his face covered in blood that she was sure wasn't just from the patient that he'd brought to her. He told her to fix him.

"He's dead." Hawk had shaken his head and told her to make him whole. "I can't do that, Sergeant. The man isn't breathing. He's gone, I'm sorry."

"You'll make him whole then."

She had no idea what he was talking about. There were others in the tent that she could be saving, should have been saving, but he held the gun to her while she still worked to try and understand him. Then his meaning hit her, and she was both appalled and pissed about it.

"You mean you want me to put him back together? For what reason would you have me waste my time in putting a dead man back into one piece? He's dead. Do you see this room? The many others, living men, who need my help?

15

And you want me to work on a man who no longer can help anyone?" The gun touched her head; it was all Mac could do not to beg him to do it, to just end her life. "I can't save him, but there are others I can."

He hit her then, took the butt of the rifle and hit her in the face with it. She was sure that he hadn't intended to kill her, but this was his way of fighting back. When she went down, she pulled out her own gun and pointed it to his knee, and watched him as he stood over her.

"Do it." She shook her head and told him to back off. "Just blow my knee out of my leg and we'll both be happier about it. I can go home, you'll go to prison, and the world will go on without us. Do it."

Instead, she got up and went to find the military police. Mac had him arrested and put in irons in minutes. The entire time, he never said a word to her or them. But it was the look, the one that told her that this wasn't finished, that terrified her. As he was being pulled away, she continued to watch his face as he stared at her like she was on his list of next to kill off.

Four days later he was out. It was then that he came to her tent. She'd not taken any notice as to who it was until it was too late. People were always going in and out of her tent, mostly nurses that needed something, like a day off. But seeing him there, with his gun pointed at her head again, Mac had begged him to kill her.

"Did you think that I'd just forget about what you did? You have no idea all the trouble you caused me. You had me arrested. I had things to do, and you nearly kept me from them." She said he'd left her no choice. "There is always a choice, and you chose the wrong one."

"Because of you and your stupidity, three men died that day. All because you wanted me to sew together a dead man by holding me hostage, while others that were injured went unattended and passed away. Why?" He stood there, the gun to her head, and waited. "What did it matter to anyone if he was whole or not? I'm here to save the living, don't you understand that?"

"His mom cared." He backed from her then, pulling the gun back a bit away from her head. "So she saw him like you left him. Blown to shit and looking like a man that had seen war. How would you have liked that?"

"We are at war, you moron. And the military would have taken care that she didn't see that. They have special duties that take care so that it doesn't happen." He nodded and then, once again, it occurred to her what he meant. She hoped more than anything that she was wrong. "His mother works in a special detail, doesn't she? She'll be the one that dresses him."

Dressing was such an odd term for what the detail did for the dead. Not only were they cleaned up, but, as best they could, care was taken so they would not look so wounded. Then, if they were going home, they were dressed in their uniform, pins and hat in place. Plastic or some other material was laid over their exposed body to keep the casket clean, if they were put in one. It wasn't dressing as in a clothing sense, but literally getting them ready for home.

"And because you were too fucking busy to do it, she saw him." Mac said she was sorry. "Not as sorry as you will be. I hope this haunts you for the rest of your life."

He tossed a picture at her, and she didn't pick it up until he was gone. It was of a woman, dressed in a surgical gown as she was most of the time, laying across a large box that bodies were shipped in and crying. Even though it was only a picture, she could almost touch her anguish, feel her pain. And Hawk had been right. It had haunted her for the rest of her days.

Forty minutes after giving herself a good talking to, she was standing over Rubin. His body was hot from the infection, his fluids down as well. Trying her best to take care of the man, giving him whatever he needed to live, she nearly sobbed when one of her nurses asked her if she was all right.

No, she wanted to scream at her, she wasn't all right. Working to remove the foot from the ankle down, she was careful of what she said to anyone. Always careful to keep her mouth shut even when she wanted to scream at everyone to leave her the fuck alone. No one would know about the hauntings that bothered her nightly.

"He'll need to have physical therapy and a nurse when he leaves here. Wait, he lives on the street. Set him up at the local nursing home, please." Her nurse said she'd take care of it as she stapled the wound closed. "Make sure that he has extra fluids as well. And see if you can find him a chess set. And a nurse or two that knows how to play."

"I'll put it on his chart." Nodding, she wrapped his wound up when she'd done all she could, knowing in her heart that it was all she could have done for him but second guessing herself all the time. "Doctor? Are you all right?"

"Yes. He's a friend and I hurt for him. He's a good man that's been dealt a crappy blow today." She hurt for them all, and knew that she had to stop this. That being a surgeon, or even a doctor, wasn't in the cards for her any longer. "I'm going to be in my office if you need me. Make sure that he has everything he needs. I'll check on him as well."

18

When she came out of the operating room, Dustin was there. She'd had no idea that anyone had been out there waiting for Rubin, so she paused in her escape to talk to him. He looked.... Well, it was hard to tell what he looked like, angry or just concerned. Since she didn't know him or his facial expressions, she assumed the former. They all felt that way when they found out about her. And Mac was sure that Lauren had told her brother what she'd done.

"Is he going to be all right?" She nodded as she pulled off her cap. "I talked to Lauren. She said that the two of you know each other."

"Yes. I know Hawk too; did she tell you?" He nodded. "I did the best I could for Rubin. You don't have to worry about that. As for the other man, I had no idea. No one told me. Not that I could have done much to help him. We were at war and there were others that needed me. I couldn't leave them to suffer like they were."

"I know that. I might not know you, but I know that."

She didn't say anything, but started to walk away when he didn't seem inclined to speak either. As soon as she moved to go to her office and type up her letter of resignation, he grabbed her hand. Why he'd done that, she had no idea. It was hot, his hand was, and she nearly moaned at the feel of it. The pain in her wrist, not from his touch but something else, made her drop to her knees. It wasn't until she was on the floor that she realized something had happened.

"Christ." The connection between them snapped as he stood there holding her. Mac didn't know what it meant, but she did know that she had to get away from him. The linking or whatever it had been made her think that this wasn't going to end well. Not for either of them. But he spoke to her, his

19

voice as strained as hers might have been had she spoken first. "You're my mate. My other half. Do you have any idea what that means for the two of us?"

"No, you can't be. We can't be. I do know what that means, but no thanks. I've got enough shit on my plate without having another McCullough in my life full time." He nodded, then smiled at her. "You don't understand, you can't be anything to me, Dustin. We're at war. Hawk and Lauren, they hate me. They'll...I'm sure you know what I did."

"I don't care."

He didn't know it all, but he would soon he promised her. Instead of telling him to forget her, she stood and turned to go to her office, lock the door, and hide for a bit. But she hit a wall, a chest like wall, which had her looking up. Hawk smiled at her, and Mac knew her life was done. Just as he opened his mouth, she let go of all her emotions and let the blackness swallow her.

Chapter 2

Hawk sat in the plastic hospital chair and tried his best not to squirm around. He was terrified that he was going to break it. He'd heard it crack and grumbled twice now, when all he'd done was stretch out his long legs. Hawk looked at Dustin when he said his name.

"You going to tell me why you're here in this room and not out in the field? Or for that matter, why my mate fainted when she saw you? Lauren said she caused you some trouble. I'd like to know what it was." Hawk didn't want to tell his brother that he'd fucked up, that he'd been wrong about what he'd done. He didn't just owe the doctor an apology; he owed her a great deal more than that. "Hawkins?"

"She doesn't like me. Not that I blame her. I was...I might have done something to hurt her feelings. No, that's wrong. I did hurt her. Not physically, though I might have a little, but I hurt her in other ways." That wasn't right either, and he shook his head. "I wasn't nice to her. I was fucking cruel to her, as a matter of fact. And before I could tell her what a

21

fool I'd been she mustered out, and I hadn't found her until Lauren called me today."

"You did something to her?" Hawk said that he had. "Will you tell me about it? I mean, if you hurt my mate, I need a good reason not to murder you where you sit."

Hawk just cocked a brow at him. Dustin was strong—all the work he did with Dad made him in better shape than most of his brothers—but Hawk was armed and knew how to kill a man with just his fingers. Instead of saying that to his little brother, he got up to pace. He thought he heard the chair sigh.

"I'll tell you what I can. But I would like to talk to her too, if you don't mind. And so you know, even if you don't want me to, I have to. I've left this for too long, and I should have known better." Dustin said nothing, but Hawk was sure that he really wanted him dead. He would, if it were his mate there on the bed. "She and I had words. Mostly me, but she was caught in my anger. Not at her—well, not initially—but I did say and do things to her that got her into trouble with a lot of folks. Including Lauren. I need to talk to her as well."

"That's not telling me anything. I know you need to talk to Mac. I understand that. But I'm fighting hard with my cat, Hawkins, and I need answers. So does he. Just start from the beginning." Hawk knew that, but that was all he had for him at the moment. "She's lying here, out cold, and all you can tell me is that you messed up? That's not helping either of us right now."

"I put a gun to her head and threatened her with certain death. Twice." Dustin stood, but sat back down. "I'm not saying that I was right or wrong, but let me explain what happened. She was a surgeon in the service—damned good one too—when I went to see her. And I was in the wrong, not her, when I did this. Grief and pain made me stupid. I wanted her to put a dead man back in one piece so that his mom, who was in special details, wouldn't see how he'd been hurt. Instead, she had me arrested."

"Okay, I can understand that. But you said you did it twice. You didn't learn anything the first time?" Dustin was the most levelheaded of all his family and would listen to him, so long as he kept explaining, kept talking, mostly taking the blame where it was properly placed this time. So Hawk leaned against the wall instead of sitting again. "Hawkins, what happened?"

He could see it like it had just happened. Hawkins tried to calm himself now. Thinking about it always made him feel like he'd lost his friend again. Every time he thought of Jack, it hurt.

"Jack and I were out on patrol. It wasn't normal—nothing is ever normal over there—but we were walking around the area and just talking. We weren't even on duty at the time. We were close to base; a hospital and a post office were within a few feet of us. Jack was laughing, his head thrown back in mirth, when he just disappeared for a few seconds. Up in the air then down to the ground right in front of me." Hawkins closed his eyes. "I didn't even make sure that we weren't being fired on yet again, but grabbed him up and ran him to the hospital. It wasn't until later that I figured out what had happened. His leg was nearly gone, his belly was open to the back. His guts were dripping—"

"Please, enough of the description." Hawk nodded, then turned to look out the window at the hospital instead of his brother. "Don't stop talking, just less gory details."

"He was dead even before I got him there, to the medical

23

unit, more than likely even before he hit the ground. Too much damage from the landmine that he'd stepped on. I knew that...someplace in the back of my head, I knew that. But he was my friend, one of the best." He watched a family get out of their car and make their way to the hospital with balloons and a small bag. They had a new baby someplace. "Mac was on duty. Actually, I think she was finished with her shift before that, but with being on base, you're pretty much on call all the time. There were wounded everywhere. Even though all the cots were filled, they were still bringing them in. But it mattered little to me. I brought Jack in and told her to fix him. This was after he was pronounced dead. She misunderstood me, and I more than likely wasn't speaking clearly. I wanted her to fix his body."

"I don't understand. I've read enough to know that there is a service that does that. Someplace the bodies are shipped to and they're cleaned and dressed, right?" Hawk nodded. "Then fixing him, you meant something else? Surely you couldn't have wanted her to work on a dead man, Hawkins."

"Yes, that's what I wanted her to do. He was a mess, and I knew it, but didn't explain to Mac that his own mom was part of the team. I don't know if she would have gotten him that way or someone would have done it for her. But she did see him. As I had. And it.... I wanted to save his mom from that, but I couldn't make, nor did I try to make, Mac understand what was going on. A few days after that, I went back to Mac. Showed Mac the picture that I snapped of Jack's mom finding her son in his box." Dustin said nothing. "I told Mac that I hoped that it would haunt her for the rest of her life...and I'm sure that it did."

"You cursed her." Hawk nodded. "And then what

happened? I'm sure that there is more to this story."

"Yes. A few days after I left Jack with his family to be sent home and buried, I went to find Mac. To tell her what a fool I'd been. I'd already spoken to Lauren; she was new to me and me her, so I had no idea that she'd go to bat for me. Mac was gone, mustered out because she could no longer be a doc to the wounded over there. Or more than likely she was afraid of people like me making demands on her that should never have happened. Lauren had her last days expedited, and I never found her after that. Not until today. And again, I fucked things up by not letting her know how profoundly sorry that I am."

Hawk watched another family clinging to one another in what he supposed was grief. The woman was clinging to the woman next to her; even from where he stood, Hawk could see her crying. When Dustin said his name, he turned to look at him and saw that Mac was awake and watching them. She was just as beautiful now as she had been. And even now she wore her anger like a shield against him. Not that he blamed her.

"I would like for you both to leave, please." Hawk sat down in the chair and Dustin moved closer to the bed. "I don't know what is going on here, nor do I care, but I really would like you to be gone."

Hawk wanted to make sure she was all right, but mostly he needed her to understand. "I need to talk to you. Please, Mac, I really want to clear the air between us." She shook her head and started to stand up. "Please. I need to talk to you about my poor behavior all those years ago."

"Look, Sergeant, you made it perfectly clear what you thought of me, and my abilities as a doctor. You also couldn't have been more true in your words when you told me that the picture you left would haunt me. I fucked up. I get it." Hawk reached for her hand, and wasn't surprised when she jerked it back. "Don't touch me."

"I was a fool." She didn't disagree, but she didn't tell him to fuck off either. "I should never have done that, nor expected you to understand. I'm sorry."

"Yes, well, so am I." She stood then and held her ground by crossing her arms over her chest and glaring at him. Hawk was impressed. She had balls, he'd give her that. "I'm leaving here. I can't do this any longer."

"The profession?" Nodding, Mac left them both standing there, just her scent to let them know that she'd been there at all. Hawk looked at Dustin. "This is my fault. I'll make it right. I promise, Dustin."

"I don't understand what's going on. Nor do I think I know everything. But you'd better, Hawkins. This, whatever it is, won't help with the three of you at odds." Hawk told him that he didn't know everything, but that he would fix it. "I'm going to go and talk to her, and you're going to figure this out. She's my mate, Hawkins. Not someone that I can have you angry with. All right?"

"Yes. I'll fix it. With Mac and Lauren. I'll make her understand that this is all on me. I swear it." He headed for the door and then turned back to talk to his little brother. "She's a good doctor. And losing her, not having her out here helping people, is going to be all my fault."

"Fix this, Hawkins. Soon, all right?" He said that he would and left the hospital. The first thing he had to do was find Lauren. He had to tell her what had really gone down that day.

~~~

Lauren looked over the file again. There was a lot of information here that she'd bet quite a few people didn't have. Like the fact that Mac had been beaten the day before Hawk had seen her. That her ribs were broken and she had fourteen stitches in her shoulder from blows to her body. Her wrist had been sprained badly and should have been in a wrap. All by her husband at the time. But Mac had gone to work, and had put in a triple shift by the looks of it. And then she'd encountered Hawk in the worst situation there could have been.

"You got time to talk to me?" She looked at Hawk, then nodded. "I wanted to talk to you about Mac. I should have done it sooner, but there just never seemed to be any time. But she's Dustin's mate and I have to make this right."

"All right, but I need to ask you something. What do you know about her? Other than you fucked up. We both did." He said a little, but not a great deal. "Did you know that she's divorced? And that she has an older brother? Also, that she's not just a surgeon, but also a brain and heart specialist as well that is called for from around the globe?"

"I knew about the divorce but not the brother. As for the medical shit, nope, didn't have a clue about that either. But it really doesn't surprise me. About her injuries, I'm assuming one of them is the one that hurt her." She asked him how he'd found that out. "When she was being treated by Boyd when she fainted a little while ago, he found evidence of bruising and a few lacerations that had been stitched up. He thinks she did it. The repair job, not the cuts."

"I don't know who it is...the brother, who is mentally handicapped, or the ex, who might be dead if he is the one

27

hurting her." Hawk sat back in his chair and she glanced at the paper in front of her before continuing. "She said that I was lazy. A few other things too, but that one stuck in my craw. Called me an ass kicker too, but before I could go all mushy on that, she called me lazy in my research. I didn't like that one bit."

"Yeah, I can see that. Lazy about what?" She told him what she'd said to her. "Me too, if we're placing blame about that. I hurt her, hunted her to go and talk to her, then I let it go. I should have done more to find her."

"I would imagine that she's been hiding herself for a while now. She only started working part-time at the hospital a few months ago. Up until then she was working as a sub for someone. When he didn't return, they asked her to work and she took on the part-time position." Hawk said nothing; he wasn't a talker any more than she was. "Dustin said that she's quitting."

"She said she was leaving her profession, yes. I don't want that to happen." Lauren said that she didn't either. "What do you think we need to do?"

"I don't know. I think, first and foremost, we find out who is taking pot shots at her. Then we figure out if we need to put him in a permanent position that makes it so he doesn't hurt her again. Then you and I will work on our groveling. I'm not good at that, in case you were wondering." Hawk said he'd find out. "Do it so that no one knows, Hawk. If she figures out we're doing this, especially now that we're in her life again, she'll bolt. And if it's all the same to you, I don't want Dustin going off too."

After she gave him the information that he needed to find the two men, she started searching for more answers. It wasn't like her to leave something half assed, and she had with this woman. Of course, she had been fighting a war, but that hadn't been a good excuse. The deeper she dug into it, the stranger things got.

"You busy, love?" She looked up at Colin, who had two children in each arm. Taking her sons, she held them while he made himself comfy on the couch. "I just spoke to Dustin. You want to fill me in on what you know?"

"And why is it you think I should know more than him?" Colin laughed. "Mac, the woman I was telling you about earlier, she's having a bad way of it. And there are things that I've found that I don't know if she's aware of. Things that might explain a few things that I wasn't aware of either."

"Yes, well, that's as clear as mud." Grinning, she sat on the other couch in her office with the boys. "Boyd knows her. Or at least of her. She's playing doctor at the ER here in town, when she's actually a world renowned brain and heart surgeon."

"I doubt she thinks of herself as playing." He said that he was kidding. "Yes, well, there might be a good reason for that as well. Her being an ER doctor and an occasional surgeon. I think she's having problems with her ex-husband, a bastard of the highest degree. She also has a brother, equally abusive, but he's also mentally handicapped. But with him, he's only violent when he's upset. When she first came back home, that was a lot. Now, from what I understand, he still has moments but not as often."

"What sort of problems does she have and how can we fix them?" Before she could answer him, Bea entered the room with them and sat on the couch, taking a baby from Colin. Rich did the same for her. Bottles were passed around as

Colin continued. "What sort of issues is she having?"

"This about Dustin's mate?" Lauren wasn't even surprised that they both knew. Rich had a way of ferreting out information better than her best man. "I'm understanding that there were some issues. You're thinking that she has more than we thought?"

"He's not an issue, but a concern at this point. And I honestly don't know if it's him or her brother. His name is Erwin, and the ex is Walton Thomas." Lauren wondered why the name seemed so familiar. "Erwin's mental capacity is about that of a six-year-old. He's just turned thirty-seven. Violent at times, especially when he's upset, and up until a few months ago was in a home that could deal with him. I don't know why he's out now, but I'm looking into it. Thomas...for some reason, I have a feeling that I've heard of him before. Anyway, he's an abusive person. Taking his inability to hold down a job out on his wife when they were married. He was discharged from the service, dishonorably, for abuse. The service doesn't take that shit lightly. But after he put her in the hospital, causing her to need surgery to put her back and arm together again, she filed for and was granted a divorce. But she's been running since."

"So basically, we only know that either her brother or ex could be hurting her, and we don't know a great deal about them." Colin smiled at her. "You know any more than this? Or could you find out names?"

"Not much more than he does about the brother, but the other, yeah. The ex-husband. Just so you know, he was Army but not all that good at it. As I said, he wasn't discharged with honors. Dishonorable hasn't helped his temper nor his sunny disposition." Lauren looked at her notes as she shifted her little boy in her arms. "Dishonored and shipped home about four years ago. I think that's why the name sounds so familiar. Anyway, about the time that Mac did her disappearing act, he was in jail. She lives now in the hotel out on Route Forty. I think she came here at first as a fill in when the ER doc that she was helping out needed time away. He's been taking a break for about three months now, but she's only just gotten her licenses to practice here."

"I talked to Boyd. He's going to have a chat with her. He would really like her to come and work with him. I don't know how she'll take that, but that's what he said. Also, I talked to the head of the surgical team at the hospital, and they said that she is well thought of as well as good at her job." Lauren nodded at Rich as he continued. "I'm to understand that there is some bad blood between you and her."

"Yes. But I'm working on that." Rich asked how. "I'm going to have to tell her I was wrong about something. I know you all will find that hard to believe, that I was wrong, but I was. Just this one time, mind you, but it's sort of making me a little teary. And she called me on it too. Just as she should have."

"You were wrong? Goodness, we'll have to build an ark, Rich. Lauren was wrong about something. Now the world will surely flood again." Lauren nearly flipped Bea off, but decided that she liked her fingers all nice and straight, not to mention still on her hands. "I would hope that you'd fix this. With her being Dustin's mate, it'll make having dinners here a little tense with this hanging between the two of you. And you know me well enough to know that I won't tolerate discord at my table, young lady."

"Yes, ma'am, I promise, it's the first thing on my list. And to find out where the two men in her life are." Rich asked if they were a problem. "I don't know for sure. The only one that would know would be Mac, and she's not talking. Not that I've asked, but I still don't think she'd tell me."

After the diapering and feeding time were done, Lauren sat at her desk again. There were any number of ways that she could find either man, but she decided that would take up too much time. So instead she made two phone calls, and within minutes she had all she needed, including the reasons that Erwin was out on his own. Colin joined her a few minutes after she put down the phone again.

"What is it?" She asked him what he meant. "You have that look on your face that tells me that you're not happy with whatever information you found. It is the ex or the brother that you're going to kill and have me bury in the backyard?"

"Neither of them. The brother is living on his own in a community that is geared up for people like him. To get them a step in the right direction toward getting their life together. He's had some issues, a few too many, and they're thinking of sticking him back in the home he was in. Not good for him or Mac since she's been keeping him paid up on his bills." Colin asked about Walton. "I know who he is."

"Is it that bad?" Laruen nodded. "Do we have to get things tighter around here again? I mean, more security or something?"

"No, I don't think that is going to be a problem. He's dead." Colin looked at her oddly. "Yeah, that's what I thought too. Until I started looking deeper into his death and the circumstances concerning it. Like, he was on a deserted highway one night and his car just spontaneously burst into flames. He was alone in the car, so no witnesses. But there

32

was a camera on the street sign that he just happened to stop in front of. Terribly convenient, don't you think?"

"I'm confused." She had him come to her computer so he could see what she was talking about. After watching the video twice, he sat down again. "So, he pulls over, doesn't get out of his car, and then it just bursts into flames. How is that possible?"

"I don't know. Neither do the cops. But here is a good one that you didn't notice, and I'm assuming that the cops didn't either. This time when you watch it, focus on the counter and not the happenings. Tell me what you see." She started it over and let him watch. When he asked for a second showing, she knew that he'd gotten it too. "Well?"

"It's been fucked with. The times are wrong, but only for a few seconds here and there." She nodded and asked him what else he'd found. "I don't know. Just the time is all I caught."

"The dates are two different days of the week. One is the twelfth, the other is the thirteenth. Whoever spliced this together was smart enough to only cut out small parts of it, so small that you'd hardly notice, and to use two different dates. The time I get, but not the dates." He asked her if she had someone who could figure it out. "Yes. It's on its way there now. There are a few other details that we should wonder about too. Like the insurance policy, as well as the benefactor. He left it all to his mom, who died when he was born."

"This is getting weirder and weirder all the time." She told him no shit. "So, we have an ex-husband that is supposed to be dead, but the records are wonky. The insurance is left to a dead woman, so there is no way she can collect, and a woman that is being beat to shit by someone we don't know.

33

You're loving this, aren't you?"

"Yes. It's a deep mystery, the kind that will keep me guessing until the very end, I hope." She watched the video again. "Why here? Why go to all this trouble when there wasn't really any reason for it? Other than the camera and the seclusion of where it is. Is he really dead? Who knows? Did he collect on the insurance by having someone play his long dead mom? If so, why? It wasn't a lot of money, just about twenty grand. I can't tell if it was collected on, nor if it was doubled because of the way he was supposedly killed. He was never a nice guy. I mean, even when I heard of him all those years ago, I knew that he was never going to amount to shit. And Mac; why is she keeping what is happening to her a big secret? Does she know that her ex is supposed to be dead and that he's really hanging around beating her to fuck? Is he even the one that we should be looking for? I have more questions than I have answers."

"You'll get them." Lauren snorted at him. "You know you will. And, I don't know if you're going to like this or not, but Mac and Dustin are coming over tomorrow night for dinner. I'm not sure who made that happen, but I think it'll be good to have everyone here, don't you?"

"Yes. I'll work on this for a little while then I'll call her. Or Dustin." Colin told her to call Dustin, Mac was still at the hospital. "All right. I can do that. Colin, Hawk and I, we really hurt this girl. I'm hoping that she won't run again. She stood up to me today...not many do that."

"No, they know better. But as for her leaving, I hope not, love. I surely don't want her out there alone either. Because we both know that if she goes, Dustin will as well." She nodded and started working again as her mate made his way to the door. "Before I forget, a man by the name of Rubin Davis is in the hospital. He was operated on by Mac, and he might know a little more about her than can be found from searches."

"I know Rubin. Yeah, I'll go see him." She wrote that down too. Her memory was getting crappier and crappier every day.

Chapter 3

Mackenzie was exhausted. She'd been called in twice last night to help the emergency room, and before she'd been able to go home early this morning, a car accident had brought her to the operating room. No rest for the weary, as her mom used to say. Opening the door to her office, she was surprised to see someone sitting at her desk...her now cleared off desk in an empty room.

"May I help you?" She knew that he was a McCullough, but not which one. He stood up and walked to her. "If you plan on adding to my already shitty day, then I'm afraid you're shit out of luck. I can't handle any more."

"No. I've come to help you move your things." She looked around and then stared at him. "All right, help you move isn't quite right since I've already done it. But I am helping you. I'm Boyd. Another McCullough, and a doctor. I'm to understand that you put in your resignation last night. Well, I've come to tell you that I have the perfect spot for you to work now."

"I don't want to be a doctor any longer. I'm sorry you

wasted your time." He grinned. "You're not all that charming, Dr. McCullough. And if you know that I'm leaving here, you also know that I have two weeks to go yet."

"Yes, I know that. And my mom thinks I'm very charming. Especially when I'm in trouble. Which, being a McCullough, isn't as often as you might think." Mac moved to her desk and leaned back in her seat. He took the room's only other chair and smiled at her. "My family are jaguars. I can smell you. The exhaustion, as well as the fact that you're bleeding, is making you weaker than normal. I would say that you've covered it well, but it's not healing the way that you had hoped and now you're not well from it. By the way, I saw you the other day. When you had your encounter with Hawkins. I'm guessing some of your stitching has pulled apart. Fine job too. I don't smell any infection, so it might be all right."

"I have been taking antibiotics. And it's really none of your business anyway." She wondered if he really could smell that she was hurt or just guessing. "I don't want to work with you."

"May I?" She nodded before she could think that showing this man, any man, that she was injured could get her into deeper shit than she was in now. "I have privileges here, but I've never had a patient come here yet. Mostly they go to the clinic that takes care of our kind. Yes, just as I thought, it's slightly infected and the stitches are pulled."

"I fell." He said nothing. His fingers touching the tender part of her back were gentle, but she was hurting by the time he asked her to stand up for him. He examined the rest of her back, surely finding that she'd missed a few places that needed seen to. "I can take care of myself."

"I can see that. And you've done a bang-up job of it so

far." He picked up her phone, and after telling someone on the other end who he was, ordered a stitch kit and some dressing. After hanging up, he looked at her. "I won't tell them who it's for, but I'll say that I need it for someone at my house. My family donates a great deal of money to the hospital here, and I can get what I need when I need it."

"I don't think it's anyone business, not even yours, what happens to me." He sat down and so did she. "You said that you wanted me to work for you. Why? And where are my things?"

"You made it very easy to move you, come to think of it. You were still packed up from your move in here. I didn't unpack all the things we took out of here, just a few items that you might want to hang. And as for me caring about what happens to you, you already know that Dustin is your mate, and that as of the moment you touched, you became my sister-in-law. So, as family, I want you to feel better. I would want you to feel better even if you weren't family, but I don't want you suffering when I can help." She told him that didn't answer her question. "That answer is simpler than you might think. There are a great many people, both human and shifters, that could use a good surgeon. Most people don't know — or care, I would imagine — that shifting while hurt badly can kill us. And if there is an obstruction, such as a knife or bullet, the cat in my case, would have the same wounds. Thus making us weaker still. I'd like to have you come and work with me so that we can prevent more deaths. As for your things, they are at your new office. Like I said, not set up, but you can do that whenever you wish."

She wasn't sure what to say or think. When the kit arrived, he thanked the person and told them that he would settle up when he went to the financial offices. Of course, he was told not to worry about it, his family did a lot for the place. When the door closed, he asked her to have a seat on his chair with her chest to the back of the seat.

Mac complied. If she was honest with herself, she was hurting a great deal more than she had let on. And she really was worried that it was infected. As she waited for him to begin, Dustin came in the room and sat on the chair that was at her desk. Ignoring him seemed to be the best way to combat her embarrassment of being half naked in from of the two men.

"The Rogers house is coming along. I did what you suggested and put in those glass front cabinets in the kitchen. It did brighten up the place." Dustin was talking like it was every day that he sat in on someone being stitched up. "The stone floor isn't what I had hoped for, but Dad likes it. He claims that it's the best-looking floor that we've ever done."

"You only put the glass on the ones nearest the window?" Dustin answered his brother that he had. "I want to see that. Maybe if I ever get around to moving into a house instead of living in an apartment, I'll have you do the same for me."

"You work on houses?" She had no idea why she asked, but it was better, she supposed, than sitting there doing nothing. Dustin told her that he did, and when she turned to look at him, she pulled her back. "Ouch."

The low growl startled her, and she turned around and looked at Dustin as he stood up and moved behind her. Boyd hadn't moved, not even to touch her again. She looked at him then at Dustin once more. This was ridiculous. Mac hated macho men. Turning around, she wanted to get up and kick Dustin in the balls. But suddenly, her back felt...well, it felt wonderfully free of pain. Even her wounds, which she knew were extensive, didn't seem to pull as badly.

"I'm not going to hurt him. Boyd hurt you inadvertently and my cat is pissy about it. But he's fine now because we know that he's only helping you." Dustin moved from behind her to face her. Then he sat on the floor in front of her. "This could go a lot easier on both of us if you'd just hold my hand while he works on you."

"I don't know why it would bother you. It's not like you could do anything about it. And it was my fault anyway." Mac did put her hand into his larger one. "Like you said, he's just making it better, not hurting me."

"Yes, we can both understand that, but you are still in pain, and while I know that Boyd didn't do it, the cat in me, who is very possessive, says differently." Mac didn't really understand, but she didn't say anything else. "Yes, we work on houses. My dad and I have been doing it for some time now. We buy cheap and sell higher. Sometimes we take on homes that people just need to have spruced up, but mostly, we're in this for a profit."

"Not much of a profit sometimes, but that's all right. You're going to feel a little pinch, Mac." She waited for it, but when she didn't feel anything until the numbness started spreading across her back, she told him he'd done well. "Yes, well, there was some added help." She looked at Dustin when Boyd nodded toward him.

"While you weren't looking, I licked your skin, the wounds back there." Mac started to ask Dustin why he'd do such a thing, but he continued before she could. "Your wounds are infected. I can heal them a great deal faster than simply stitching them up. Boyd is going to do that too, just in case I missed something, but you'll not be getting any sicker from it."

"I'm confused." Dustin said he understood that. "Do you? How can you when I don't even understand this myself? All this.... You have come into my life and turned it upside down. I've been moved to an office that I had no idea was even around. I'm to be a partner to a person that I don't really know. You claim that I'm your mate, and I already have a very terrible relationship with two of your family members. I have.... Well, that isn't any of your business, but my life isn't what I want it to be. It hasn't been for a very long time."

"Did you know that your ex-husband is alive?" She stared at him, her heart racing as she looked at the door then back, wondering how quickly she could leave before he came to her. "You didn't know, but suspected it, I'm guessing."

"He...he's still around?" Her heart hurt. Fear of him, of what he would do to her, made her feel like she needed to run. Or just let him finish the job he'd started so long ago. Dustin asked her how she'd figured it out. "The accident was too pat. Too out in the open. I didn't say anything to anyone at the time. I just...I guess that I didn't want to feel stupid or paranoid if I was wrong. Are you sure?"

"Yes, we think so. And that's what Lauren said about it too. She's investigating it." Mac asked him why. "Because of what you called her. So you know, she isn't pissed at you any longer. Neither is my brother Hawkins. He'd like to speak to you about what he did to you."

"He didn't make my life any better. Neither did Lauren." Dustin said he knew that, and so did they. "We were at war. There were wounded and dying everywhere. I'd worked for seventy-two hours straight, and still they kept coming in.

Then he brings me this man who was.... He wanted me to fix him."

"Hawkins told me. He said that he was cruel to you. That he should have never let his anger and grief do that to you. Either time." She nodded, not sure where this was going. "I'm sorry too. That this is overwhelming you, but if Walton is out there, and you didn't know it, who is hurting you?"

It was on the tip of her tongue to tell him. Just let someone else know what the hell was really going on in her life, but she asked Boyd if he was finished and he said that he was. Standing up, she pulled her shirt back on, then her lab coat. There wasn't anything to tell them, she assured herself, and changed the subject.

"I have rounds to make, if you gentlemen are finished here." Boyd laughed as he packed up the kit he'd used. "And I'd like for you to bring me my things back before I call security in for theft."

"It won't work. I mean, you can call them, but it won't do you a bit of good." When Boyd was finished, he leaned over and kissed her on the cheek. "Welcome to the family, Mac. I'm glad that you're going to be joining us."

Then he left. Dustin was still on the floor, but she had a feeling that he could be up and in her face in seconds. Instead of running, which she wanted to do in the worst sort of way, she sat down and tried her best to look bored and calm.

"Your brother, Erwin, he's not doing well in his program, is he?" She wanted to sob, just wanted to curl into a ball and cry until there was nothing left in her. "I have some friends that can help you out with him. I know of a clinic that isn't state funded, and they can give him better care than he can where he is now."

"He's not capable of learning anything. I mean, just to get him to remember to dress himself and to use the bathroom is a struggle for him." Dustin stretched out his long legs, and she closed her eyes at what the simple movement did for her body. "When he was home, living with my parents and me, he had a temper. Then when they both passed away, he lived with Walton and me when we were home and in-between tours. It wasn't until then that I found out that it wasn't a temper, but he was having a reaction to the meds that they had him on. They were hurting his head."

"And no one tried to figure that out?" She said it was more that no one cared enough to figure it out. "Who is doing this to you? I think we've ruled out your ex and brother, the only two people that I know of that might have done it."

"And if I said to you 'it's none of your business,' you're going to look anyway, aren't you?" He said he would. Or Lauren would. "It's none of either of your business. And I'd appreciate it if you just stayed out of my life."

"Your life is mine now." She said nothing and stood up. Leaving him on the floor, she made her way to the door. But him saying her name, softly, had her turning again and looking at him. "Because I took some of your blood in me, I can tell your emotions as well as talk to you through a link. If you need me, you only have to think of me and I'll answer. Or come to you."

Saying nothing, she left. Whatever was going on in his head, he would have to deal with it on his own. Mac was going to finish out her two weeks, get her things back, and move on. It was all she could do at this point.

~~~

Dustin held the cabinet while his dad anchored it to the

wall. He wanted to sit down and have a nice cold glass of beer, but they were behind. But thankfully, having Randy fired and not needing someone to watch him all the time, they were beginning to see light at the end of the tunnel. Dustin hadn't realized how much Randy had screwed up until he was gone.

"You and I, we're going to have to talk about this girl of yours." He told Dad that she wasn't his yet. "Well, you gonna work on that?"

"Yes. When she trusts me. I don't know that I'd be so trusting either if I was her, but I'm working on that too." Dad asked him what he meant. "Someone is hurting her. While we all thought it was her ex, she didn't react like she knew he was alive, so I think we can rule him out. And her brother didn't make her terrified. More like she was hurting for him. Sadness, not fear, was in her mind when she talked about him."

"So who is it?" Dustin said he didn't know but he was working on that too. "You sure do have a lot of irons in the fire, son. You know that we're here if you need us. Nobody needs this, and especially someone that is going to be a part of this family."

"I know that too, Dad." They hung the next three cabinets and he got down off the ladder. "I have to finish up my house now, I guess. I've just been putting things off until we had the time to go do it. And I'm happy that there was enough work to keep me from it, but it's been a project house long enough."

"No kidding." He laughed with his dad. "I do like what you've done to the decking. Nice touch adding that old stone we took from the other house. But now, while you're in the mood to get it done, we should bring Mac around and let her look at some of the other finished projects to get an idea what she might want."

"You're right. Great idea. And the stone…well, it seemed a waste to just throw it out. And this way, I can see how long it'll last out in our winter months before we use the rest of it like that." Dad said he hoped it worked because Mom wanted some of it. "She's more than welcome to whatever we have."

"Yes, she knows that too. By the way, there is a shipment of old furniture coming in tomorrow to be stored in that old barn we have. I guess your mom made a deal with those sellers in town. I tried to tell them that this town isn't strong enough to support a shop that has expensive old stuff in it. But they didn't listen, and now we got us an empty store again."

"What about that idea that you had? About putting in a parts store for restorers? Most of that stuff can be shipped. A door or two wouldn't be that hard to wrap up. And we're forever finding old doorknobs and stuff when we work on the houses. What do you think?" Dad nodded, but didn't say anything. "You've already started on it, haven't you?"

"Your mom, she thought it would be a good thing for her to do all day. Since she's got her nose in what we do anyway, I figured she'd be there and not on every project we do." Dustin asked him if he believed that would keep her away. "No, I don't, but it would be a nice change for her."

Dustin thought his dad was nuts but kept that to himself. He loved mom coming around, and she had some excellent ideas. As they started finishing up the kitchen, all he could think about was Mac. He knew she was having a hard day. Every emotion that she had seemed to roll over him too. And the grief that she felt made him want to find her and hold her. When he felt a nudging in his mind, he paused in painting the trim over the cabinets.

Can you really hear me? Dustin told Mac that he could. *I have an issue here. A big.... Can you come here? At the hospital. And bring one or two of those large brothers of yours.*

I'll be there in five minutes. We're just down the street. She thanked him, but he could feel her fear. Profound fear. *Are you safe?*

Yes. For now. Hurry.

He told his dad where he was going and why. Calling to his other brothers, he told them to meet him at the hospital. Not only was Lauren in town, but so was Josh; correcting himself, he thought of his new name, Jon. Things were about to get hairy, he thought.

Jon and Lauren were there before him. Dustin didn't want to get in the way of whatever was going on, but he did go to stand as close as he could to Mac. The man standing with a gun to her head made him want to kill. But he also didn't want to make the man pissy and hurt her.

"Dustin, this is James Winder. He doesn't know what he's doing." The man snarled at Mac that he did too fucking know what he was doing. "Drugs. He's here to get me to give him drugs. Like every other fucking bastard I know."

It was a strange thing to say, and her anger was palpable. Dustin looked at the man and knew that he was as high as he'd ever seen a man. Dangerous too. Dustin asked him what he wanted.

"She won't tell me where she's got them." It was then that Dustin noticed that James was bleeding, profusely. "I got me a terrible pain, and she said that I can't have none until I tell her what I got in me. I want them now."

"Understandable, but I'm sure you know, being on drugs, that there are certain kinds that don't mix well together.

47

Perhaps she's trying to save your miserable life." James growled again. "I don't know if you're aware of this or not, but you're growling at the wrong person. I'm not in the mood to explain to you why, either."

"She has them here. It's a hospital, ain't it?" Dustin said it was, but only to help people. "Well, she ain't helping me. I'm bleeding really bad, and she's holding out on me."

"Again, I think she's only trying to save you. Fat lot of good that's going to do you. I'm going to kill you, you know that, right?" The man stared at him. "Yes, and you know why too. She's my mate, and you're going to die because you caused her fear. If you so much as cut her finger, I'm going to tear you apart so that your own mother won't know it was you."

"I just wanted something to make me feel better." Dustin moved closer to the two of them. "You can't be coming up on me like this. I have a gun. And I ain't afraid to use it on whoever I need to so that I can feel better."

"You might have a gun, but that's nothing compared to what I am. I am a cat...guns might hurt me, but you have to know that I'm here as well as my entire family. You're so fucked right now." Colin moved behind the man and Mac just as he took another step forward. "Put the gun down right now and I'll only muss you up a bit."

"I need it." Dustin told him that being dead wasn't going to help anyone. "Just tell her to give them to me. Then I'll go away."

"No. I'm not going to make her do a damned thing. She's already told you no, I'm assuming." Mac said that she had. "See? You should have taken her at her word and you'd be able to walk out of here unharmed. Now, as it is right this moment, you're going to be dead. Is that what you want?"

"Yes." Dustin had already figured that out when the man continued on his path against the odds. "I hurt all the time. If this is what it takes, then so be it. I can't be hurting like this again."

Before he could ask the man if he'd tried to get help, Boyd walked up to him from behind, stuck him in the neck with a needle, and James dropped like a log. Colin took his gun and Dustin took Mac into his arms. His cat wanted to kill, but he calmed the moment that he touched Mac.

"He was going to kill me. Just so that someone would kill him." Dustin told Mac he knew that. "He wanted to die? He wanted you to come here and kill him? How fucking stupid is that?"

"Very. Now let me hold you a little tighter, please. Otherwise my cat is going to come out and kill the man anyway." Dustin was so glad when she wrapped her arms around him. Picking her up, he carried her to the hallway and to the elevator. Kissing her throat, mouth, and shoulders, he nearly came in his pants when she wrapped her fingers into his hair and held him to her. The ride up had literally nearly become that, her riding his cock while he took her hard against the elevator wall.

Her office was unlocked, thankfully. As soon as he was inside the room and the door closed behind them, he pressed her to the wall. Tearing at her clothing was only making him needier. His cat was snarling at him to take her.

"I need you." He laughed and told her that was not even close to what he wanted. "I know this is a mistake, but Christ, I'm on fire with need. Please, fill me."

He couldn't. Not until his cat had his fill. Stripping down

to nothing, he let him take him and pawed the rest of her clothing off. As soon as her pussy was bare for them, his cat moved in and licked her cream.

"Oh my God."

She came quickly and his cat purred his approval. The second, then third time that she came, his cat nudged her legs wider apart and fucked her with his tongue. Dustin felt his need to mark her, his overwhelming love for this woman. And when he let him go, Dustin took her hips in his hands and pulled her to him to finish what his cat had started. She tasted like heaven.

"Please. I need you to fuck me." Standing up after giving her another quick climax, he lifted her up, her legs on either side of his hips. Watching her face, he slid into her slowly, feeling each muscle along her sheath grip and hold him. "Please, Dustin. Please."

There wasn't any way for him to hold back. He felt his own climax slide over his skin, his body ready to empty. When she nuzzled his neck then bit down on his throat, Dustin came so hard that he saw stars. His body powered through two extraordinary releases before he tilted her neck to the side and sunk his teeth in hard enough to draw blood.

Christ. Dustin came again as she cried out her own release, and he held her to him. Mine, was all his mind kept saying. His cat too. She was theirs, and he knew that from now on, she was his to protect too.

Chapter 4

Trying her best not to be embarrassed, Mac tugged at the shirt that she had put on, as well as pulling up her pants once more. There hadn't been any scrubs in her size when she'd been called to the ER again, and she was sure that everyone that came near her could tell that she'd just had the most mind-blowing sex anyone had ever had. Especially her.

And it didn't help that Boyd kept laughing. It wasn't really loud, but it was enough to make her want to pick up something and imbed it in his forehead. She asked him again what had happened. When he stalled too long, Mac picked up the water bottle and glared at him. Of course, that did nothing to stem his laughter.

"Mr. Walsh was mowing his lawn when he claims that something came out of the sky and hit him in the head." Mr. Walsh assured them both that he wasn't lying. But even she could smell the alcohol on his breath. "He said that he thinks it was an alien ship that was full of foreigners and that they probed him."

"Probed him where?" The man pointed to his penis, which to her looked as if he had run the mower over himself. "And this examination, did they say anything to you? I mean, what was their purpose in probing you there in that bit of yourself?"

"Ain't no bit when I'm ready, lady. I'm fit like a bull." She felt her face heat up again. Boyd told him to behave himself. "No man likes to be told that he's only a bit. I can use it when I wanna and they don't complain none."

"I'm sure that they don't. But what I was asking you was, what reason did they give you to probe that part of your body?" She didn't look at Boyd, but she had a feeling that he was laughing at her or the two of them. Clearing her throat, she spoke to Mr. Walsh again. "Mr. Walsh, I can't help you if you don't talk to me."

"Well, they said they were a measuring me." She didn't say anything, not even sure she wanted him to continue. "I guess they're gonna make themselves have one of these dicks, and they needed to know what size they wanted."

"I see." She didn't, but continued after clearing her throat again. "And with this probing they did to you, they had to... hmm...shave you?"

"I wasn't sure what they were doing, so I might have wiggled a little." She nodded and looked at the cuts that weren't that deep on his groin. "Lady, you keep touching me like that and you're going to see my bit."

She should have been used to it. Should have just marked it down as one of those days. But her temper wasn't in the best of places, Mac was exhausted, and she didn't for one minute believe that he'd been probed.

"You calm that erection, or so help me I'll give you

soft peter to make it so that you never get a hard-on again. Not even with the best of probes. You understand me?" He nodded and she looked at his dick again. "I would suggest that the next time they want to shave you, to probe any part of you, that you have them use some sort of electric shaver, or at least put some lotion on the area when they're done."

"Yes, ma'am. I was wondering, too, if you could perhaps look at my hole." She looked at him and watched his face pale. "Never mind. I'll just put some lotion back there too. I think it'll be better on my butt if'n I do."

As she walked away, removing her gloves as she went, she was stopped by the police who were still there. But Boyd saved her, or them, by telling them that she had an emergency elsewhere, if they could please wait. She'd completely forgotten about the incident earlier with the drug guy. Escaping to her office was her only recourse right now.

Her office was empty of Dustin. She was both disappointed and glad that he was gone. And when she found the envelope with her name on it, she sat down and held it to her chest. Whatever he could say to her right now was not going to be an improvement on her temper. She didn't know why she thought that, but not opening it was better, she thought. Then she tore it open.

"Darling." Well, that was certainly a good start. "I'm so sorry that I had to run off like I did, but I have several men at a job site that are doing nothing until I get there. I am truly sorry that I can't be with you, bringing you back to our home and making you come several more times. I love the way you scream out my name. With all my heart, Dustin."

Putting the letter back into the envelope, she sat there for several minutes. If asked, she wasn't sure that she could have told anyone, even under threat of death, what she'd been thinking about, but when her door opened she looked at the man that had been terrorizing her for most of her adult life, and if she was honest in her thinking, he'd been bothering her since his supposed death as well.

"What do you want?" He sauntered in, his body much larger than it had been years ago, and sat down across from her. "I don't want you to come here anymore. Besides, I thought you were dead. That's what I hoped for, anyway."

"Isn't that just too fucking bad? And you know what I want, darling...what I always want." After having Dustin call her darling, this time seemed so much dirtier. Like she was being insulted rather than cherished. "So, what do you have for me? I'm hoping nothing. It thrills me to no end to have to beat it out of you."

"I've met someone." He laughed at her; she was sure that he didn't believe a word that she said. "He and I are getting married. I don't want you to hurt me anymore, because I've figured out that it's been you all along, hasn't it? You've hired someone, or a lot of someones, to do what you couldn't. Beating me up hasn't gotten you or them anything but a record. I want you to call them off, right now."

"Again, like I give a shit what it is you want. You know why I'm here. And I think it's about time that you started giving me what I want, not what I have to take from you." She looked at the door when someone knocked then opened it. Mac didn't know the young man there, but was glad to see him. "You'll have to come back later. Dr. Gibson is busy."

"I'm Jon. My parents are Parker and Reese. You know me." She nodded, desperate for any help she could get, even from a young man. "Mom sent me to find you so that you could give me a lift home. I have to get going now, Aunt Mac. I have a ton of homework to do."

She stood up and so did her tormentor. Instead of sitting back down, as he told her to do, she made her escape out the door with Jon. They were nearly to the elevator doors when her name was called.

"This isn't over." She nodded, knowing full well that it wasn't. "I'm going to get what I want, Mac. I always do. By any means. Remember that when you're driving the kid to his home. Someone could just come out of nowhere, like they have been lately, and knock you around a little. Fun for them and a little for me, but now that you know I'm around, then I can enjoy it too. Just know that I'm not going to go easy on you now."

Not remembering how she'd gotten in her car, she looked at Jon. Then without saying a word to him, she burst into tears, sobbing big gulps of air into her lungs and crying them out when she needed to breathe.

"I have you now." Nodding, she continued to cry. "I'm sorry to have lied to you, but I thought you could use some help. My parents have no idea that I'm here."

"He was going to hurt me again." Jon said that he knew that. "I thought he was dead. His buddies, they were still coming around, and I thought maybe they didn't know that he was dead. Or worse yet, that they knew he was alive and he was sending them because he was in hiding. I don't ever give drugs to anyone…it's why I'm getting beaten up all the time. I think he knows that too, that I'm only there for their entertainment."

"You are." She nodded, then looked at him. "I'm not going to lie to you right now when I tell you that I'm not human. I'm way more than any shifter, too."

"I don't understand." He put out his hand and a ball of fire appeared. "You can make fire? I don't know a lot about shifters, but that seems to be a pretty unsafe and useless talent."

"It's very useful when I can breathe it on my enemies as a dragon." She looked at him and he laughed. "I would never do that to you; with you being a mate to one of my family, I will never harm you. And I have much more control over my powers, too."

"You can really be a dragon?" He shifted into one in that moment. Tiny, yes. But when he blew a flame over her glove box, she could see the benefits of flames. Trust, like she had for Dustin for some reason, washed over her. Like a warm sunshiny day on a beach kind of peace. "You're going to fix that, right?"

He became Jon again, ran his hand over the scorched place, and smiled at her. It was as good as new...much nicer actually, than it had been before. When Mac asked him what he was, he settled back on the seat and spoke.

"I was...I guess you could say that I was created. By men who thought that having a weapon—because that is what I am in the wrong hands—would give them a great deal of notoriety and fame. I would be very financially beneficial to them had they finished their work and turned me against mankind somehow. There are things you must understand about me. I can read your mind. Feel your fear, love, emotions of all kinds. Also, it's a simple thing for me to go from one point to the other with just a thought. I can become anything, anything at all, should I need to, and I have so much magic that I'm still figuring some of it out." There wasn't one thought

56

that entered her head at that moment. "I've overwhelmed you."

"Yes." Since her hands weren't shaking as badly, she started her car and backed out of her parking space. "What you saw in there, it wasn't what you think. I didn't know.... I thought that he was.... I'm not sure what you thought I was doing, but I wasn't going to let him hurt me again."

"Remember, Aunt Mac, I can read your mind. You thought he was going to hurt you and you were going to let him." She drove for a few miles, trying hard to think of how to explain this to him. "He had it in his head to kill you this time. The irony of it, being killed in a hospital, made him laugh. He does want you dead now. Does anyone else know that your ex-husband is trying to kill you?"

~~~

Dustin knew that Mac was upset, he just didn't know what about. As she walked through the house that he and his dad were working on, he tried to make small talk with her, and gave up when she didn't respond. He wondered what had happened.

Dad came into the kitchen just as they were looking in the pantry. "I have those locks you wanted. I think you had a good one there what with putting those.... Well, hello Mac. I didn't know you were about."

"I had some trouble at work, as you know, and when I left today, they asked me to take my two weeks' notice at home. Which is fine by me. I just have to figure out what to do with my life now." Dad glanced at him and he shook his head no. He didn't want his dad asking about working with Boyd. "This is a really good job, Mr. McCullough. I'd live here if I had the money."

Dustin thought that was an odd thing to say. As a doctor, he assumed that she'd have money. He wondered if in addition to being beaten up, someone was taking her checks as well. It bore looking into. Then he remembered that she was taking care of her brother's needs. He also knew, from Lauren, that it was expensive. He listened to his dad explain to Mac what they'd started with in the house.

"It was a real fixer upper, let me tell you. Nearly had to start with just the studs. We even put on a second floor to the place, just because it's a nice starter home. It only had the one bedroom when we started, and a little bitty bathroom that I could hardly stand in." Dad showed her that the pantry now had a walk-in freezer, something that they'd been putting in homes for a year or so now. "That way if a little family wants to buy them a side of beef or something, they don't have to worry about not having the space for it. And we put in a little garden in the back, filled with herbs. You cook?"

"I do. Not like I've heard that Reese does, but yes, I can do more than boil water." Dad laughed and they both looked at Dustin. "Do you?"

"Yes. Mom said that if we were going to eat her and Dad out of house and home, the least we could do is pick up the slack occasionally. Mom does not cook. She's better at organizing someone else to do it for her. Or going out." They all three laughed. "Mom signed us up for cooking classes during the summers and we really enjoyed them. While I'm not as good as Reese either, I can whip up a nice pot roast with all the trimmings, and bake a nice loaf of bread if I want."

"This kitchen looks like something out of a magazine. You know, one of those specialized cooking ones? I just realized this must be the Rogers home. I heard you telling Boyd that he suggested you do glass fronted cabinets. It looks good. I really like it." Dad told her that their kitchen had every kind of gadget. "I don't have a home. I mean, right now I live in a hotel room that's smaller than this kitchen. But it serves, I guess. For now."

"You have a home now." Dad looked at him and then back at Mac before continuing. "I guess the two of you need to talk about things."

"We do." Dad wandered off, laying the locks for the pantry on the counter. Picking up the electric screwdriver, Dustin told her what he was doing. "There are any number of reasons to have a lock on the doors here. Mostly for children getting in and out of the room and into the freezer. But I like the added safety of all the food items in here that could be harmful to some—"

"Jon came to see me today. Did he tell you what happened?" He said that he'd not talked to Jon today. "He came in my office when I had a visitor. Not anyone that I had invited or knew was around, but he was there to threaten me."

Dustin nearly gouged the wood when the tool slipped. Putting it down carefully, he turned to her. Letting out a long slow breath, he didn't want to upset her any more than he was sure she already was, so he smiled.

"And he threatened you how? The reason I ask is because I want to know if I should make him suffer or just kill him outright." He saw the tears then. They traveled over her lovely cheeks and his heart broke for her. Pulling her into his arms, he held her. "I love you, Mac. I'm so sorry. Talk to me. Tell me what's going on."

"My.... It was Walton. You said that he was alive and now he's here. He's...since I was in grad school he's been chasing after this dream of being something huge. I just never realized that it was going to be a drug lord and I was going to be supplying him with the stuff." He didn't ask. He wanted to ask her if she had provided Walton with drugs in the past, but she answered before he could. "He was forever coming into the unit when I was working. There weren't a lot of drugs out of the country, but there were a few places that we could get them from. Walton even tried this scam on me about how he'd gotten hurt and needed something for the pain. When that didn't work after the first time, he went to my colleagues, other doctors and units, to try and get what he wanted. It got to the point where he was hurting himself for the drugs. Once he used a bayonet on himself so that someone would supply him with drugs and refills. Then.... Well, I thought he was dead. When you told me that day, I thought you had to be wrong. Hoped that you were wrong about him being alive, but you were right. Why would he do such a thing? Then he came and there he was, starting all over again."

"Is he the one hitting you?" She told him that it hadn't been him since he died, but the people who did it told her it was from him. "I see. And I'm guessing that this is the reason that you quit the hospital. Along with my family harassing you, you can't have had an easy time of it. Could you?"

"Your family was the least of my problems back then. So therefore – and you know this – we can't be together." He didn't point out that they already were. "Your sister-in-law might say she will get along with me, but we both know that she's scary mean. And Hawk? He terrifies me. What if I do something that pisses him off again, and this time he pulls the trigger? At this point in my life, I might care that he does. But...well, I am just so tired all the time from being stressed about all this. I love being a doctor, but it's so hard when every day you have to fight with someone about it."

"Okay, first of all, Lauren likes you. And, I might add, she's impressed that you made her think about some things. Such as being lazy about figuring out what had really happened that day." She groaned and he laughed. "Believe it or not, she doesn't have too many people stand up to her and tell her that she's wrong about something."

"I doubt that made her like me. It more than likely had her call someone. I don't know, the president or something." He just stared at her. "Please tell me that she doesn't know the president of the fucking United States. Tell me. Please?"

"She's known him for a long time. Even before he became president. He's been to our house a couple of times when—" She put her hand over his mouth and he grinned behind it. Kissing her palm, he pulled it away and kissed her on the mouth. "Okay, we'll not talk about the people she's connected to. And Hawkins as well."

She moved around the kitchen, touching the new handles on the cabinets, pulling out the empty drawers. Mac paused in front of the second sink and ran her fingers over the concrete counters before turning back to him.

"It's not been him that hurts me, as I said. But he is connected to the beatings, I know that now. Over the last month, I've been caught twice on my way home from work, and three times just outside of the place I'm staying. It's a nice hotel, but not very secure." Dustin decided that he was going to have better security put in at their home, today if he could. "They wanted drugs. No different than the man from earlier today, but Walton is less nice about it, believe it or not. Yes, he did have a gun that he threatened me with before. And yes, he has one now. And if you're going to ask, yes, he had visited me, or had someone visit me, the day that Hawk came to see me."

"You were hurt badly. Lauren found the paperwork on it. Yet you stayed on duty and worked a long shift." She said it was her job. "I can see that, yes, but you were hurt and exhausted, and then my brother comes along and does what he did to you."

"I left the service after that. Or, I put in for a transfer and was given my walking papers. Not dishonorably, as I could have been, but I was mustered out all the same. I found out later that it was because of Hawk's CO. Lauren." Dustin nodded. "I was close to my time anyway. I hated to leave, but it was for the best."

"Perhaps, but I'm sure that they could have used your talent. I understand why you did it and my family is responsible. About your ex, have you called the police? Let them know what is going on?" Mac nodded and moved around the kitchen again. "Okay. So why is he still out and about? There has to be a good reason that he'd show himself after everyone thinks that he's dead."

"I don't know. When he was 'alive' he would always have witnesses to why he couldn't have been where I said he was. The restraining order never worked with him. Then after he was declared dead, it wasn't necessary to have it kept up with. The other men, I never knew who they were. Not that I think that would have done any good anyway. Plus, I think that Walton gets a sick perversion from harming me." Dustin finished up the lock and put the tools away while she continued. "Just before you came into my life, I had an encounter with one of his friends. He beat me with a whip, a cat-of-nine tails I think it's called, while I was strapped to the front of his car. I think his plan had been to run me down when he'd had his fun, but someone spotted his car, and he didn't want to take the chance of killing me and someone remembering his plate number. His words, not mine."

"Christ." She nodded. "And today, when Jon came by, I'm assuming that Walton wanted drugs as well as to knock you around a little. And after all this time, with his death still out there, he thought he could just start over."

"Yes, but Jon said he was there to kill me. That the irony of me being killed in a hospital was not lost on him." Dustin felt his cat roll over his skin, and how he wanted to make the man pay. "Now you can see why it's not a good idea for me to be with you. I understand that you're a cat, but even they can't outrun a bullet or being attacked by some of the things that I've been hurt with."

"He's going to pay, you have to be aware of that." She said that he would, but not at the expense of one of his family. "Oh, we're not going to be hurt by him. This I can guarantee you. He's going to suffer too. Maybe not at my hands, but someone's. And then he'll leave you alone. Permanently."

"You're not listening. Try thinking with your head. This man isn't like others. It's as if he's on a mission or something. And he's very willing and able to kill me. If he won't stop until that happens, I'm pretty sure he won't hesitate to do the same to you. At times I couldn't have cared less if I died, but I just can't do this anymore." Dustin smiled at her. "You look scary mean right now."

"I am. Scary, I mean. And he is going to pay, Mac. By the way, I'd very much like to call you Mackenzie, if you don't mind. I love that name, and you're so not a Mac." She rolled her eyes at him and Dustin laughed. "You're so beautiful when you're upset. You know that, don't you?"

"No, but you're insane." He agreed with her and pulled her into his arms. "As much as I'd like for you to leave me to my own devices, I do love you holding me like this. It's very.... Well, it's very comforting and warming."

"I love holding you as well. Especially when you're naked and riding me." She pulled back and looked at him, shock all over her face. "Of course, I could show you how much I like it by letting you ride me when we get home."

"I don't know what to do." He nodded, telling her that he understood that. "I'm glad that one of us does. I know nothing about you, other than a few things, yet I feel very safe and loved by you."

Before he could tell her that he did really love her, her cell phone rang. He knew immediately that the hospital needed her. She was barking orders into the phone even as he pulled her gently along with him to his car. It was a short drive to the hospital, and he was going to stay with her until whatever she was doing was finished. Boyd contacted him a few minutes later.

I'm assuming that Mac is with you? He told him that she was on the phone with the hospital now. *Good. There is a ten-year-old coming in with a single gunshot wound to the head. He's conscious, but that could change in a minute. Someone has to remove it for him so that he can live to talk about it.*

She's on her way. Are you going to be there too? He said that he was going to assist. *All right. Keep an eye on her and I'll rest easy. Also, I'm going to talk to Lauren. I have some information.*

I'll see you both there.

Chapter 5

Lauren had Reese look at the pictures that had been sent to her. They weren't in the best of shape, but they were telling. Reese handed them to Jon. They were going over some of the information that Dustin had given her, as well as what Jon had found out on his own.

"The man in the picture, as you have guessed, isn't Walton Thomas." Lauren asked Jon who it was. "He was a homeless man that had been hired to drive the car to that point and wait for someone to pick him up. I've had contact with a couple of people that he hung around with, and they think that he's made it so good on this job that he's flush now. He's dead, and was assumed to be Walton when his charred body was found in Walton's car."

Lauren looked at Reese. "What did you see in the pictures that I might have missed?" Reese laughed and said she doubted that Lauren missed a damned thing. "Maybe, but I'd like to be sure. They're coming here for dinner tonight, and I want to make things better between us."

"She is afraid of you. Most people are that don't know you well." Jon laughed when she snorted at him. "I'm not one of those people. I know that you're a big mushy baby too."

"You show anyone that video that you took of me rocking my sons and I'll murder you in your sleep." They all three laughed. Lauren knew that there wasn't any way for anyone to kill the young man if they wanted. And anyone who tried would, more than likely, end up dead themselves. "What can I do to make her less fearful of me and more like family? By the way, I went in and talked to a friend of hers, Rubin Davis. I met him once, a long time ago, when his grandson was killed. He said that since she's been his doctor, he knows she's been hurt a great deal. But she rarely mentions it, nor does he pry. I think he pries a great deal, but doesn't get answers."

"I'd say that this is a step in the right direction. And she's paying for Rubin to go into a nursing home when he's released too. I just found that out when doing a search on the hospital. If she leaves there, the hospital will lose a great deal of income from her name. And if they do, then they're done. The hospital is running on a short income. As for what I see in these photos, there is a tattoo on his arm." Lauren took the picture back. She had missed that, thinking it was a smudge on the photo. "Can you get that cleaned up a little more? To me, it looks like an American flag, but it's hard to tell. We'll need to have more than Jon's say on that being Walton, even if he is walking around like he owns the world."

"I have someone going over them now cleaning them up. This photo, along with the others, was taken off a recording of the autopsy. The recording is being worked on as well. There is voice, but like the other things we've gotten, they've been doctored." Reese asked what kind of connections this man had if he could do that. "That's what I'd like to know."

"Miss?" They all turned to the doorway where the butler was. He smiled at them and said that a visitor, Dr. Gibson, was here. She told him to show her in and bring some snacks. "Very good. Also, might I suggest that dinner be moved up a little? I have heard from the other households that they're coming here now as well."

"Good idea. Thanks." She waited for Mac to come in, and wasn't surprised to see that she was pissy. Or standoffish. Either way, Lauren had her work cut out for her. "Mac, I'm not sure if you've meet Reese, but she's Jon's mom."

"I have. The other day." She sat down when asked to, but she was as stiff as a board. "I'm not sure what you think I can give to this search thing, but Dustin said you wanted me to come by early. I wanted to tell you first off that I'm not going to put up with your shit."

"I should hope not." That seemed to take the wind out of her sails or the shit out of her oatmeal, whichever. But she did look a little confused. Lauren continued. "Hawk was called away so he won't be able to be here tonight, but I'm to tell you that he and I, we have your back on this. And your front and sides should it come to that. We both fucked you over, and I, for one, am sorry. I should have, as you pointed out to me, gotten all the details before assuming. I hate when people do that to me, and I hate myself even more that I did it to you. I am sorry."

She watched the woman. Lauren decided that she'd never play poker with her. Her face was unreadable and blank. Colin walked in with their daughters, one of them screaming at the top of her lungs about something, and he handed her to Mac. And when she shut up and stared at her, Lauren laughed.

"I think she's either shocked or getting to know you." Mac said she had a way with babies for some reason. And when she turned the baby over with her belly across her legs, Lauren started to point out that she hated that when she burped, then passed gas. "What the fuck was that all about?"

"They only cry like that when they're hungry or hurting. And since I know you'd never starve your children, it had to be pain. So burping sounded good. As for the other, I can only assume that she had gas built up at both ends." Picking her up again, she smiled. "I heard that you have four children. What's her name?"

"That one is Beatrix, this is Abbie. The boys, which my parents are currently bathing, are Caleb and David. In order of birth, their names are the alphabet." Colin laughed as he continued. "There are days when I can't tell which is which except for males and females, but we try our best to keep them straight." He asked what was going on.

"Your wife is trying to tell me how she messed up. I'm not sure that I think she was wholly at fault, but I'm willing to let it go if she does. Hawkins? I'm not so sure. He.... I have to talk to him." Lauren was all right with that. She supposed, really, it was all she could hope for right now. But she would be there when she talked to Hawk, if only because she wanted to hear him grovel. "I wanted to talk to you anyway, before everyone came for dinner. I've decided to work with Boyd. I've not told him yet. I want him to make sure that he wants me to work for him still. After this morning, I'm not sure about too much."

"I heard from the staff at the hospital. They said that you did a wonderful job on Joey." Colin told her what he'd heard, but Lauren watched Mac. She was much like her in that moment, not comfortable with compliments. "His mom and dad are, of course, ecstatic, and currently working with the police to see why the other little boy had the gun. But he's doing well, I'm told. Thank you."

As she sat there, Lauren glanced down at the papers and noticed something else. Picking it up, she asked Mac to look at it. "Tell me what you see here, please?"

The copy was of the autopsy report. It was clearly written and the marks on the paper were right where they should have been, she thought. But there was something wrong with it. At least she thought so. When Mac handed it back to her, Lauren asked her what she saw.

"Several things. First of all, while it looks like it's fully filled out, it's far from it. There is a cause of death, but it says pending after it. There is no stamp on it, and even if you only got a copy from someone, there should be a visible stamp saying that someone signed off on it. Also, and this is really a concern, there is no name, no file number, nor is there a name of the doctor or coroner that performed it." That was a lot more than Laruen had seen. "You need a copy of one that is filled out to compare it with. Or, in this case, someone that has filled them out before. I can get you one for future reference if you want it."

"No, having you is more than enough. All this, the things you pointed out, why would I have this and it not be completed? I mean, I really don't know." Mac took it back and asked if she could write on it. "Yes, please do."

"See this blank? That is supposed to have a number in it. To tell where and when it was performed. As in which office and state. There is also supposed to be a mark here, a doctor's stamp with his license number on it. This one tells me who did the procedure, as well as anyone that might have been present when it was done. Since there are no marks, there is no one to go back on to find out. Also, and this is the really bad part, the cause of death. Yes, it has one, but it's dependent on toxicology reports. After all this time, there should have been an attachment to it to explain what, if anything, was found. I'm assuming that this is the paperwork that was supposed to be about Walton, correct?"

"Yes, it is. So, even though this was filed, it's still no good to anyone unless they had the full report. What would cause this to be left undone?" She told her. "You think it's been tampered with? I'm assuming not just because it's not filled out right."

"Yes. That's part of it. But the hospital or offices are required by law to make sure that these are done in a timely manner. For insurance purposes, courts if there is a problem, and wills to be read. I'm thinking that somewhere between the time it was filed and when you got this copy, someone went in and replaced the original with, perhaps a copy that was used for notes during the procedure." She asked her if she did that, made a second copy. "No. I record what I find, then put it on the paperwork when I'm finished. I think a lot of newer doctors do. That was someone old school who wrote their notes directly on the paper to be redone later."

"That would narrow it down, I think." Mac told her not necessarily. "Why not? And you know, some good news would help a great deal right now."

"Oh, I can help you with who did it. The man that wrote that is Dr. Howard Shine. But he's been dead for about six years now. I know this because he was one of my internships when I was in grad school. And he couldn't have done that before he died because he was blind from an automobile accident he had about a month after I graduated." She picked it up again and smiled. "I'd say that this is something that was in another file for another dead man. There is no mention of any tattoos or burns on the body. Walton had two. Neither of them a flag, but a name of some old girlfriend...Bambi, I think her name was. And mother was spelled with an a, not an o. Blunt force trauma isn't what supposedly killed Walton. Fire was."

Lauren was impressed. Humbly so. Dustin had arrived while they were talking, and when Mac sat down and took his hand into hers, Lauren thought she was either coming to terms with all of them or she was as afraid as she had been earlier. But given all that, she'd made a great deal of headway into finding her ex. And Lauren was going to enjoy taking the man to task when she did.

~~~

Bea handed the bowl of mashed potatoes to her eldest. He took it, but didn't move out of the kitchen as she'd thought he would. Instead, he stood there staring at her as if he was going to tell her something. Bea had no idea what it might be, but she waited on him.

"I need a job." She didn't tell him that he really didn't need a job, nor did he need the money. He knew that. So Bea did what she knew he needed and asked him what it was he wanted to do. "I want to work with Dustin and Dad. I have as much experience as they do, I know that. But I need to do something. Staying with the kids all day...I love them to pieces, but I need to talk to an adult too. I forget how adults act, Mom. That's not good, is it?"

"No, I wouldn't think so, but I understand." He smiled.

71

"But don't think because I understand means that I'm agreeing with you. You have a responsibility, one that you cannot slack on. Those children need their parents. And since you were the one that insisted you could be a stay at home dad, then that lays at your doorstep." He nodded, looking so crestfallen that she wanted to tell him she was sorry. "What will you do with them all day if you get called to work?"

"I don't know. I've not thought that far ahead. But everyone else is working. Even you and Dad. All I do each day is answer the phone and troubleshoot." She asked him if he was good at it. "Yes, very good, but I don't get to see anyone. I need....Mom, I need stimulation. With people my own age."

Laughing would have hurt his feelings, she knew this, but she did smile at him. There was so much of his father in Colin, more than she wanted to admit sometimes. So turning her back to him so that she could smile bigger, she asked him what Lauren had said.

"She said that if I found someone that could care for the children as well as I do, then that would be all right with her. I know that it's going to be hard, but I am in serious need of the outdoors. Something to not just flex my brain on, but my muscles too. My cat is wanting to play more too." Bea asked him what he'd done so far. "I was hoping you could help me. I know that I'm going to be terrible at interviewing someone. I'm going to do background checks out the butt on them. Also, I don't know what sort of questions to ask of a potential nanny. Or two. I think two would be better, don't you?"

"Yes, I do. I know you have that woman that helps out sometimes. You should start with her. She might have someone in mind as well." He nodded, smiling now. "Take the potatoes in the dining room, Colin, and I'll give it some thought."

He left and she giggled. Rich asked what was going on when he came in to get a serving bowl too. After telling him what was happening, he sighed heavily.

"I was afraid he was going to ask us to do it full time. I love those babies, but they plumb wear me out." She said they did her too. "I know he'd do a good job working for us, what with him doing it all that time before he went to college. But I'm telling you, love, I'd rather do four houses than watch those babies full time. I think they're harder on this old man than housework is."

Handing out the rest of the platters and bowls that the cook had prepared, she joined her family in the dining room. It was just about the same size as the one they had at their own house. Bea had thought at one time that it was just big enough for them and their growing sons. Now she wasn't so sure it could take one more chair added to the table. With babies now, and hopefully more coming, wives added to the mix too, she would need a new room and table if they were going to get together as a family. Smiling, she looked at her mate.

"We need to remodel, I think." He told her that he'd been thinking the same thing. "Bigger everything, I'm thinking. Couches and chairs. We'll need high chairs and cribs. Oh Rich, this is going to be so good for us. Don't you think?"

"I do, love. I really do." Dinner was loud and friendly. "You think any of our kids will ever think to tone it down a bit? My goodness, they're a loud group, aren't they?"

Nodding with a smile, she looked around the room. Even though there were arguments, she knew they were all in good fun. Even poor Mac, who seemed to be just as strong as the rest of the women in their family, appeared to let herself go a bit and join in. But she could see that she was terrified of something.

"She's afraid that Hawkins is going to come through the door at any moment." She asked Reese why. "You need to hear the whole story, I think. They are not on the best of terms. I don't know that she trusts Lauren all that much either. Tolerates her, but there isn't any trust from her. And believe it or not, I think it hurts Lauren's feelings."

Bea could see that. Lauren, for all her toughness, was tender too. Why, just the other day she'd seen her sobbing over one of the girls when her little sock had gotten lost. It was getting harder and harder for Lauren to leave them when she had to work.

Getting to the bottom of it might be hard. Hawkins was as closed mouth as anyone she'd ever met, and he was her son. There were times when she didn't know what he was up to, but this needed to be fixed. And now. Reaching out to her son, she asked him if he had time to talk to her.

Yes, but not long, Mom. I'm sorry about missing dinner. I did tell you I might get called out. She said she understood that. *I love you.*

I love you as well. I want to know what you're doing to fix this between you and Mac. What a name, Mac. Sounds as if she should be a truck or something. Well? He laughed and she felt his humor all the way to her heart. *I don't know what happened between the two of you, but it needs to be taken care of.*

I agree, but since she's afraid to be near me, and for good reason, it's been difficult for me to talk to her. Bea asked him what he'd done. *I put a gun to her head and demanded that she do something that was well beyond what was her job requirement. I was angry and grief stricken. And my temper wasn't at a good place.*

A gun to her head? I'm assuming you can't tell me what happened. He did, in great detail. *Oh Hawkins. What a thing to ask of someone. I know you had the best of intentions at heart, but those other men, the living, they needed her too. Could it not have waited a moment or two?*

Yes. He was silent and she could feel his pain. *I have done a great many things that I shouldn't have, Mom. And a good many that I hated to do. But what I did to her, asked her to do for me, it's the thing that keeps me awake at night. Makes me wish I could do it all over. For her, not for me. I was a terrible person to her.*

She told him he wasn't terrible to anyone, but knew that in his heart he would still believe that he was, no matter what she said. When he told her that he had to close their connection now, she let him, but her heart hurt for her son. He was much like Lauren, strong to and for others, but they were in a great deal of pain too. She would have to work on that.

Clean up was done by the boys. Jon helped too, but he didn't participate in the conversation as much as the others did. Bea moved in and out of the kitchen, pretending to make a plate of cookies and fruit for her girls and a pot of tea for them to enjoy. Boyd stopped her by putting his hands over hers.

"We're not going to talk about anything that you need to hear." She nodded and leaned her head on his shoulder. "Oh, Mom. Whatever would we do if we didn't have you around to make sure we walked the line?"

"I'm sure that you'd do just fine. Not as well as I'd have to tell you, but I'm sure that you'd do it right." Kissing him on the cheek, she smiled up at him. "When are you going to convince that girl to come and work with you?"

"I was hoping you could push her in the right direction." She smacked him on the shoulder. "Well, Mom, you have to admit, you're good at pushing people into things that they'd normally not do."

"I'm not entirely sure how to take that, young man." He kissed her again and she glared at him. "Boyd Wayne McCullough, you will not use that considerable charm on your mother. I will have your respect."

"Forever."

She believed him and made her way into the living room. She was sure that she'd been bamboozled, but she loved him too much to point out that she was much smarter than him. Especially when it came to maneuvering around people.

When she walked into the room, her hands laden with food, she could tell that she'd missed something. And it wasn't a good thing. Lauren had a look of pure hot anger on her face, and Mac's wasn't any better. However, Reese was laughing, so she sat next to her, handing her the bowl of fruit. She asked her what she'd missed.

"Well, Mac took exception to Lauren telling her that she wasn't good in a fight, and she showed her that she's quite handy with a blade. I'll pay for the damage to the floor, by the way. So when she threw it at her — the blade, not the floor — it landed no more than a hairsbreadth from Lauren's foot." Reese ate a handful of grapes. "Then when Lauren thought to retaliate, Mac tossed her to the floor…again, damages I'll pay for. Lauren thought she'd better sit —"

"You're not helping." Bea looked at Lauren. "She got the better of me because I let her. I didn't want her hurt."

"Sure you did. And I'm guessing that you moved your

foot closer to the knife so that I'd feel better about myself too?" Lauren growled at Mac. "Why don't we go three out of four? This time I might be able to hit you in that flapping mouth of yours."

They both faced off, and Bea stood up and started tapping her foot and crossed her arms over her chest. Neither woman looked at her. She was surprised, because that was all it took for the boys to turn in her direction and tell her that they were done. When she cleared her throat, it was Lauren that looked away first, and that was when it happened.

The room was filled with the sound of breaking glass and popping sounds. She wasn't sure what was going on, but when she hit the floor with Mac atop her, she started to rise. This was no way to treat her.

"Stay there before you get your fool head shot off." Shot? Bea didn't move, but she felt the fear now. Someone was shooting at them. Her sons and mate came in the room then, most of them cats, and Lauren barked at them to stay out. Something was flowing into Bea's eyes, and it took her a moment to realize she was bleeding.

Honey, don't move. She told Rich that she wasn't planning on it. *The pack is looking for the shooter. You just stay where you are for a moment longer.*

I don't hurt right now, Rich, but I do have a little blood on my face. He said that he could see it and he was coming. *You get yourself shot and I will never forgive you. Can you not hear me talking to you? That means that I'm all right. You stay right there and let these girls handle it.*

Jon is out there. That made her afraid and glad at the same time. *He said that he's found the man and is bringing him to us. Don't die on me, sweetheart. I can't stand the thought of being without you.*

I'm all right. She was beginning to feel a little lightheaded, but didn't say so to Rich. There was enough to worry about right now. When she opened her eyes and looked up at Mac, she could see worry on her face. She also realized that she was no longer in a house but an operating room. "I'm not well, am I child?"

"No, ma'am, you're not. But I have you now. I want you to take some deep breaths for me." She felt something touch her face and she inhaled to speak to her again and felt her body just float. In seconds she gave up and just closed her eyes.

Chapter 6

Dustin wasn't good at waiting, and thought he was spending way too much time at hospitals. Today...today was the worst yet. His mom was in surgery. She'd been shot by a madman.

"She'll be just fine." Dustin nodded at his dad. "I love her to pieces. She can't be leaving me all alone in this world. I just don't know what I'm going to do if something happens to her. She's my world, next to you boys."

"I know that she's in good hands. Mac wouldn't let anything happen to her." He knew that she'd not let it happen, but that didn't mean that it wouldn't. His mom was literally in his mate's hands. He looked at Hawkins when he came into the room with them. Hugging him tightly, they all moved together to surround him, to give him support as they'd been doing for each other.

"What happened?" Colin told him they'd been at the house and someone had fired upon them. "Do we know who?"

79

"Yes. He's in a jail cell for now. Jon is watching over him. It's Mac's brother, but she doesn't know that yet. We don't think he did this on his own." Colin looked at Dustin as he continued. "He was told to shoot into the house. Not who to shoot or why. He doesn't seem to understand why he's in trouble, either."

"He's handicapped." Dustin nodded at Hawkins. "I'm assuming that since she doesn't know then she hasn't spoken to him either."

"Mom was hurt and she started working on her before the ambulance arrived. They said had she not been there that Mom would never have made it as far as she has. Mac was in a zone and didn't seem to notice anything but Mom." Hawkins nodded at him. "I haven't asked her anything either. I don't want to mess with her concentration. The bullet, we were told, is very close to her heart."

Hawkins sat down. Dustin just noticed that he was in fatigues. Not only that, but he was sure that he was wearing a vest under his shirt...a flak jacket, he supposed it was called. Being armed the way that he appeared, Dustin had a feeling that his brother had come straight out of the field and to here. When he noticed that he was looking at him, he smiled.

"When you told me what happened, I jumped on the first travel going out. It just happened to be a nice vampire that just happened to be in the area. Victoria said I had to come as I was or not at all. For some reason, I got the feeling that she liked the fact that I was sweaty and armed." Victoria appeared in the room with them and asked to talk to Lauren. "She's going to help Mom, if Mac will let her."

"I can talk to her if you want." Hawkins said it would have to be Dustin, because she didn't trust him or Lauren.

"All right. I'll tell her who and what she is. Hopefully she can see her way past being pissed at you and let her help."

Victoria followed him down the hall. No one asked them where they were going, and he figured that was because of her. As soon as they were outside the operating room, he could hear the music. It was loud and very bass. He looked at Victoria and reached out to Mac.

I don't have time. I'm.... I don't think she's going to make it, Dustin. He started to tell her that there was someone there to help when Victoria simply entered the big room. He followed, not sure what was going to happen, but he needed to make sure that Mac allowed the extra help that Victoria could give them. "I know you."

"Yes, I'm here to help Bea. She and her family are very good friends of mine. Have you removed the bullet?" She said that she had, but Bea was bleeding too much. "I can help. The rest of the staff, they'll not interfere."

The room was quiet now, the stereo muted but still playing. The bars on the system wrapped in plastic were still moving. Someone—more than likely the old vampire—had stilled all movements of the staff. But before she could step forward, the machines all around his mom went off. The heartrate was flatlined. In seconds, less than that, he knew that his mom had died.

"Hurry." Victoria nodded at Mac and opened her wrist. Instead of putting it over his mom's mouth, as he had assumed that she'd do, she let her blood drip right into her open chest cavity. The room tilted a little, and he had to grab onto something or fall. But Dustin watched them both as they worked against the clock. "You'll have to assist."

They worked together, Victoria and Mac. Almost before

she was asking for a piece of equipment, it was in her hands. Then after a few more minutes of that, they didn't speak, neither of them wasting time on words when there was work to be done.

On some level, he knew that he shouldn't be in here. That he wasn't dressed for this sort of thing. Mac and her still crew were dressed in scrubs; gloves covered their hands all the way to the elbows. And blood was everywhere.

He stepped back when one of the staff moved. They were helping now, no one mentioning that he was there, nor that Victoria was assisting. Dustin wasn't sure that they even noticed the other woman...they were as focused on Mom as Mac was. When the machine that had screamed at them started to beep again, he thought it was over, that she was going to live. But they both worked harder...stayed the course, as his dad was fond of saying.

It was an hour later, maybe more, when they both stepped back. He didn't move from his place, just continued to watch the monitors and the people there. The beeping was steady now, the room a bit more relaxed. Mac thanked Victoria as the mask was moved off Mom's face and once again, she was given vampire blood. The spike in the beeping startled him, but no one else moved so he assumed it was all right.

"You're very good at this." Mac thanked Victoria and told her she was as well. "Yes, well, I've done my fair share of helping with the wounded when necessary. But you're better than good, my dear, I would say that you're the best there is."

"I had help." Victoria looked at him and winked. "We'll move Bea to recovery in a little while and see about getting her to lie still for a few more days. She's lost a great deal of blood and has had some major trauma too."

Dustin moved into the hallway with Victoria. He wasn't sure where they needed to go now, but when they were a few short feet from the waiting room, he stopped her. He needed to know, not that he would necessarily share it all.

"She was as good as dead when she was brought in here, you know that." He nodded. "I helped, but Mac saved her. Yes, my blood helped. But without the proper procedures, such as closing off the tiniest of openings in her chest, she would have bled out anyway. No amount of blood that I could give her would have done any good had it just leaked out into her body." Dustin felt lightheaded again. "Stand tall, young Dustin. You have a mate that is going to need you more than you could ever imagine when she is done with this. It's going to hit her hard that she just had to do open heart surgery on your mother, and that someone dear to you all nearly died."

"She's thinking of quitting this line of work." Victoria told him not to let her. "I can't stop her any more than I think you could. Even with your magic."

"No. If she's ready to quit, I won't be able to stop her. But today...I think that today restored her faith in herself. Do you know who shot Bea?" He told her. "I'm going to visit him. I won't harm him, but I will find out what I can."

"Jon said that his head is a jumble. He's handicapped." Victoria said that she'd get who had sent him. "He might think that his brother-in-law is dead. We know now that he is not."

When Victoria left him, he moved into the waiting room. His family stood up and he told him everything he had witnessed, holding nothing back from them. When he was finished, he sat; it was that or fall flat on his face. His dad sat by him and asked if Mom was really going to be all right.

"Yes. She can't shift for a few days. I know that she's going to be stubborn about that, so you'll have to make her." Dad said that he'd do that if he had to sit on her. "And she'll need to rest. A great deal. What I saw in there, Dad, I think that Victoria was right, Mackenzie is the best there is at this. She was.... It was like I was watching a miracle happen right before my eyes."

"It was one. I tell you, when your mom told me she was bleeding but all right, I just knew she had no idea that she was bleeding on her chest. It was pooling around her like she'd had a bath in it." Dustin held his dad when he sobbed. "I owe Mackenzie so much. She gave us back your mom, my mate, and I don't think I'll ever be able to repay her for that."

"I don't think she'll see it that way, Dad." Dad nodded. "We'll be able to go see her in a little while. They're moving her to recovery soon. But I'm going to take Mackenzie home. Victoria said she was going to need to rest and unwind."

"You do that. Take care of my girl for me. And you tell her, in case I don't get to right away, that I will be beholden to her forever. You tell her just that way for me." He said that he would, and stood up when one of the nurses that had been in the operating room came to talk to them.

"Dr. Gibson will be out shortly. She said to tell you that everything went well and that she expects a full recovery." They all shouted and smiled. "I'm sure she heard you. If you all would wait just a little longer, as I said, she'll be out to speak to you and to answer any questions."

Dustin sat down and decided he was going to ask her to marry him, just as soon as he got her home. After another half an hour, she came out to talk to them, but instead of talking, she was hugged and told how much they loved her. Dustin waited his turn. He'd show her how much he loved her too, when he got her home.

~~~

Mac liked the oversized tub, but she thought that the waterfall that poured fresh water into a koi tank beside it was spectacular. As she laid in the tub, trying to relax, she watched the fish moving around the tank and felt better than she had in the last few hours.

"How are you doing?" Smiling at Dustin, she told him she was doing much better. "Yes, well, so am I, now that you're here. Can I join you?"

"Yes, I'd like that very much." He took off his shirt and put it in the hamper. She laughed at that. "Do all your brothers do that? Put things away when you could easily just leave it on the floor?"

"You've met my mother, haven't you? Does she strike you as the type of mom that would be all right with us being lazy about a clothing hamper?" She grinned bigger. "Not to mention, when we leave a table, we clear our things plus one more item, and we always clean up the kitchen, as a group, when dinner is done. Mom might not cook, but she runs a tight kitchen. It's what made us so romantic."

"Romantic? By clearing a table?" He said it was a very important lesson. "I suppose. I'm still seeing her there, her chest covered in blood, her face smeared with it. I don't think I'll ever forget that."

"Me either. And for now, let's not talk about it, shall we?" She moved so that he could join her in the tub. His cock was already straining from his groin, and when he moved in behind her, wrapping his legs over hers, she felt it at her back. "Now. We're going to sit here and talk about us. Nothing bad or scary, just get to know each other."

"I'm not sure I can do that with you naked in here with me." He told her to behave. "I'm trying, but you're so manly."

"I love you." She nodded. "I know that it's much too soon for you to feel that way about me, but I wanted you to know that for as long as I'm alive, you will be my first and only true love."

"I don't know if I love you yet. I feel a great deal for you. I love things about you and how you make me feel, but I don't know if that's love." He took her left hand into his and kissed it. "You make me feel like I'm worthy. I'm not entirely sure of what, but I feel that way."

When her hand was placed over her chest, she noticed the ring. Sitting up, she turned to look at him and he kissed her. Not a quick kiss, but a powerfully consuming one. She asked him about the ring.

"It was my grandmother's. She wasn't a nice person... not really, I guess. But for some reason she liked me a great deal. I think it was because I was the baby, and she knew that I would be her last grandchild. I don't know. Anyway, right before she died, she gave this to me. I was about ten or so, and thought that a girly ring was not all that good of a gift." Mac told him she thought it was beautiful. "It is. And it looks fantastic on your hand. I've not done this right, but I wanted to tell you what she said to me. She said, 'Dustin, there will be times when pretty girls will come into your life and you'll think, this is the one. But don't be thinking with your twig and berries, use your heart.' Yes, we had that sort of relationship. 'When she comes along, you give her this ring because I'm giving it to you with all the love I have to offer you. You tell her that. You make her the best and most important thing in

86

your life. Because you will only get the one chance to make a good first impression on your mate.'"

"What a lovely story." He kissed her again, leaving her thinking that his grandma had had it right. You only got one chance and this was hers. "I think perhaps you've changed my mind. I do love you, with all I have to offer you."

"Will you marry me, Mackenzie? Be my wife, my partner, and the mother of my children? You do want some, don't you?" She nodded and turned around in his lap. "Good. And someday, when you're ready, I'd like to convert you to a cat. You'd be my beautiful jaguar."

"We have so much going on right now." She leaned her forehead onto his. "I feel, right now, that I can do this... whatever it is with Walton. But to be honest with you, I'd like for you to make love to me."

"With you. I want to make love with you." He kissed her then, the taste of his need and his love right there for her. And when he pulled back, she looked at him and could see not only his sincerity, but his passion and love too. "I love you, Mackenzie. And will forever."

The tub was big, but not big enough to make love in. She thought about a hot tub, something for just the two of them, and decided to ask him about it. As he lifted her out of the still warm water, she went to him willingly. This was a man that she knew instinctively would never hurt her.

The bed had arrived only today. It was huge, specially made to hold his longer frame. And when he laid her upon it, she felt the expensive sheets against her back, the full pillows under her head. Money could buy these things, but love was what had made him purchase them for her.

"You're so beautiful. My cat needs to mark you."

Before she could ask what he meant by that, he shifted, the big jaguar standing near the bed and looking at her with big dark eyes. Spreading her legs for him, she cried out when he licked her, and nearly fainted when he slid his tongue deep inside her.

He loves your taste. The cream that you're sharing with him is making him very happy. She told Dustin he was making her happy as well. *Just wait until I have my turn. You're going to scream so much you'll be speechless in the morning.*

A challenge she was willing to take on. But even as that thought occurred to her, she did scream. The releases, several in quick succession of the last, nearly brought her to the darkness. True to his word, when Dustin took his body back, she did scream more than she had in...well, forever.

His hands touched her everywhere. Each time his mouth ran over her flesh, his tongue felt as if he were scorching her. His teeth nipped painfully at her skin, but his mouth would make the tiny hurt feel better. Then when he slid into her, she held her breath. It wasn't like before, but so much more.

"I love you." She nodded, unable to speak. "You're mine, Mackenzie. I want you to know that. You are mine forever."

"I love you too, so much."

Her breath felt like it was being taken from her when he moved. Her body was on a ledge, and she wasn't sure that she wanted to fall over it. And just as she was about to tell him no more, that her body couldn't take it, he bit down on her throat and she came hard enough that stars sparkled behind her eyelids, and her heart stopped beating for several seconds.

"Come for me." She shook her head, even though her body was screaming yes, she could. And when she did, it was stronger than before, like her entire being was being twisted up. The pressure was let out, her body dropped to the bed only to be lifted up again and again. Each time he tossed her a little higher, her body wrung out more. Until he came.

Mac felt his climax as it touched off parts of her that she'd not had any idea were attached to her body. Her ears rang, her hair crackled under the extremeness of it. And when Dustin dropped atop her, she couldn't have moved even if the house were on fire. She was sure that if they did find her that they'd be amazed at the smile on her face. One that she could feel all over her body.

Dustin rolled off her just as she was drifting to sleep. His soft snore made her sigh. These were sounds she could get used to. And a warmth that she could hold to her heart until her dying day. Relaxing into slumber, she heard him tell her that he loved her, and she didn't have it in her to answer. Mac let the welcoming darkness take her.

The room was dark when she woke. She was alone in the bed, but knew that Dustin wasn't far. Getting up, she pulled on a robe and made her way down the stairs. His dad and brother were in the kitchen with Dustin when she entered. After the night that she'd had, she didn't want to spoil it with bad news, but asked if everything was all right.

"Yes. I was just at the hospital. They said they tried to call you but your phone is off or something." She glanced at Dustin when he said he had turned it off. "Thought so. Anyway, Bea is doing well. I talked to her a good long time. She's gonna do as you tell her. I promise."

Mac nodded and started filling the empty glasses with more tea. She was nervous, if she was truthful with herself, and she was sure that Dustin knew it. He pulled the pitcher from her and asked her to have a seat.

"I don't know if I want to." He said things were fine. "If you say so. But it's four in the morning and you three have been down here for a while. What is it you don't want to tell me?"

"Nothing bad, I promise. Your student loans are paid off. The credit cards that you used for it are also paid off. And your brother is going to go to a place that can help him once this is over. We're not pressing charges, by the way." She asked him what he'd done. "I'm sorry. I thought you knew. He was the one that shot up the house."

"No." She sat down hard and then found herself with her head between her knees. "He wouldn't have done something like that. I wasn't even aware that he'd been released. Where is he?"

"He's at the hospital for now, under observation and to visit...he wanted to see my mom and we took him there. He didn't do anything wrong when we were able to talk to him, not when we found out what had happened." Sitting up, she asked Rich what had happened. "Your ex-husband, he went to see him and had him released. We're working on how that happened, so you know. But he told him that the house was an old and abandoned, so he could have fun with it. He thought it was a special time with Walton, after everyone told him that he'd been dead. I'm not sure, after talking to him, that he ever cared for Walton, but he wanted them to be friends so he did it. He regrets it now, let me tell you."

"So, he lured him to that house with the promise that he could fire a gun. A gun that, I might add, nearly killed someone." She started to cry then, it was simply too much. "I'd like to see him, please? He...I need to talk to him."

"All right, honey. I'll take you there tomorrow. Today he's

still being taken care of. All right?" She stood up and Dustin smiled. "Right after you dress, we'll head into town and get the other stuff taken care of, like your name on a couple of accounts. And there are a few other things that we need to get finished up too. You up for that?"

Nodding, she kissed him and felt better about everything. As she left the kitchen, her face hot with embarrassment, she thought of her ex and brother. Walton wasn't going to get away with this, not this time. Erwin wasn't going to be taken advantage of again. Not so long as she had breath in her body.

Chapter 7

The realtor showed him and his dad around the house again. Dustin had some questions, about a thousand right now, but he wasn't sure that she'd be able to answer them. First of all, they had nothing to do with the house to make it sellable. It was perfect. And secondly, he wanted to know why the owners were selling so cheap. The house wasn't in that bad of shape. But Dustin didn't want to be told again that she'd find out. For a realtor, she was certainly uninformed.

"And you're telling us that this house is going on the market tomorrow for only twenty grand. Just twenty." She nodded at Dad after consulting her notes. Again. "Why would they do a fool thing like that?"

"I'm sure I can find out for you, Mr. McCullough." She handed him a flyer, one that she'd given them both twice now. Dad gave it to him to add to the stack. "The stats on the house are right there. The year it was built and —"

"I got all that the first time you told me. Darling, do you show houses for a living? Or are we your first?" She started crying then and spilled out the entire reason why she was there. "I see. You don't worry yourself none. We'll get to the bottom of this."

She'd been sent there by her boss, a man who they had dealt with before and someone that neither of them trusted all that much. Ben Creamery had decided that he was simply too busy to take them to a house they were going to make more profit from than he was. Then he decided to get them into trouble by lowballing a house and getting them to buy it. Apparently, he thought that he could flip houses and make the kind of money they were, and told the girl to tell them a much lower price on the house and then turn them in for stealing the house. Like that was going to work. Dustin thought the man was off his rocker, but said nothing.

"The flyer says how much the house is really going for. I thought if I handed you enough of them, then you'd see it and ask. Mr. Creamery told me several times that I wasn't to say anything about the price except the twenty grand that I told you about. And if you found out, that he'd take the blame." Dustin asked her if she trusted her boss. "No, not since I've been working there. Oh, he was all right at first, but lately he's been talking like he hates us all, and you guys especially. I don't care if I lose my job or my pending license at this point. I just wanted to make some extra money for the holidays for my family."

"You won't lose your job. I promise." Dustin said nothing. His dad would make sure that she had employment and was paid more for her help in this. "Now, I'm going to call the police, but not on you. We'll get to the bottom of this right now."

Dustin moved around the house again while his dad took

care of things. It was a good buy at the asking price. Even all the appliances were included. He decided to purchase it anyway, just to have as an investment. While he was thinking of the few little improvements that needed to be made, he thought of Hawkins. This would be perfect for him.

I have a house for you. Hawkins said he wasn't looking for one. *Yeah, but you will. I know you only have a few years to go with the Army, and you're going to need a place to settle up in. This one is perfect for you.*

Still, I don't want a house. Ignoring him, Dustin described the house. *What the fuck would I want with seventy acres?*

To be alone. Hawkins was quiet then. *It butts right up against the nature preserve, so you won't have any neighbors across from you. To your left is a mountain that looks like solid stone. And a lake too, if you're inclined to do some fishing.*

I like to fish. Haven't done it in a while, but I could fish again. Where is it? He told him. *That's not too far from town and you guys. But far enough that you'd not be coming by every ten seconds. How's the house?*

I have in mind to upgrade the kitchen for you. And you could use a bigger garage. Perhaps a barn too. He asked him why. *To hide the bodies in. Christ, Hawkins, you'll need a tractor. I don't know what you'd do with it other than that.*

Bodies are better buried in the yard. That way the grass is always greener. Dustin wasn't sure if he was kidding or not, and decided that he didn't want to know. *I don't even own a stick of furniture, Dustin. Seriously, what the hell am I gonna put in it besides a bunk?*

Mom just bought a bunch of furniture from one of the antique stores in town. Are you for that sort of thing? He said that he liked old stuff. *Good. Then I'll put some in here for you. After I paint it. So? You want it? If you don't later, sell it. I'm sure you can make a hefty profit off it.*

Yeah, buy it. I have the money in a couple of accounts. Not having anything all these years, it's given me a nice bit of cash I can work with. And with Larson investing it, I've got a bit. He cautioned him about paying cash. *I guess. Just go ahead and get me the best price for it, and I'll make arrangements with Larson to purchase it. All right?*

Yes. Where are you? No answer, so he let it go. *Hawkins, when will you be coming home for good? You know that we all miss you. And you still have to talk to Mackenzie.*

I'll be home in a couple of days. She's going to be first on my list to talk to. And so you know, I've done a few things for her too. Shit, I know that she's gonna hate it. I talked to the president. He's getting her back pay for after she got out, and a few medals too. So, you're gonna have to sparkle up when he gives them to her at the White House soon. That wasn't going to go over well, he knew it. *Also, you should know that I have a couple of friends looking after our dead man. Thomas isn't going to be long for this world when this is done. She has to know that.*

I'll talk to her. He said that would be good. *Hawkins, I love you. I really do miss you too. Be safe.*

I always am, little brother. He heard laughter and it made him smile. *Dustin, do me a favor, will you? When you have a couple of kids of your own, I want you to keep them out of the service. At all costs.*

I'll do that. Hawkins told him good deal. *All right, I'll get the house for you and fix the things we talked about. Barn or no barn?*

After Hawk told him to put a big one in, he closed the connection. Turning around in the room, he realized that he'd

96

been so focused on talking to his brother, he'd missed a few things. The police were talking to the young woman, and Dad was helping. He would hate to be Mr. Creamery right now.

Calling the bank while everything was being dealt with, he put in a really low offer. Before he could give a phone number to reach him at, Mr. Carson accepted. He told Dustin that it had been on their books as a foreclosure for a long time, and said that he had told his wife today that the first offer he got, he was accepting. Dustin had gotten a much better deal than he'd ever thought.

By the time he'd made arrangements with Larson about the house, he'd set up his crew to come in and do the work. There really wasn't much to be done, so he knew he could spare the men for a couple of days. Then he had someone come out and give estimates on the barn to be built. All in all, Dustin thought it was a good day.

Going back to the jobsite after talking with the police, Dad told him how he'd hired Becky to work in their offices. Dustin laughed.

"You do know that we don't have an office, right?" Dad said he was taking care of that too. "I see. Anything else I should be aware of now that we have a secretary?"

"Yes. As you said, she's gonna need an office someplace. I was thinking that one downtown. That old warehouse on Fifth." Dustin said that it would be perfect. "Yeah, that's what I was thinking too. We've been done working on it for a bit now, and it's just sitting there. Might show a few people how good a job we can do when we set our minds to it."

He told him how he'd contacted Hawkins about the house and his call with the bank. "I'm going to have a crew go out after the sale is done and have them spruce it up some.

And the lawn taken care of." Dad asked about the barn. "I've called one place to give an estimate, but if you know someone else, you can call them too."

"I think you can handle this. I like that you're gonna have it all ready for him with that stuff your mom bought. That way we don't have to haul it all away, and someone will get some use out of it." Dustin drove them in their truck into the driveway of the project and stared at the house. "It looks good, don't you think?"

"I do. I love the colors too. Mom had that about right, don't you think?" Dad nodded. "You should take some pictures of it and show her when you go see her tonight. I'll be in later too, but I have to sit down with the banker about some paperwork for Mackenzie. Plus, making arrangements for us to be married."

"She said yes?" Dustin told him she had. "Well, that's about the best news I've had all day. I'll tell your mom. No, you tell her. She'll be tickled pink, I tell you. Best news all day."

When the day was finished up and Dustin was on his way home, he thought of Mackenzie. He'd been thinking of her all day, actually, but now it was what he wanted to do to her when he got home. As soon as he pulled in the driveway and got out of the truck, he could smell food cooking. Following his nose, he walked out onto the deck where she was standing over the grill with a large fork in her hand.

"Mackenzie?" She turned and smiled at him, and he felt like a huge weight had been lifted off his shoulders. "You put the grill together."

"Well, let's just stay I started on it. The instructions aren't as easy to understand as I thought they might be. I mean—

and this was said to me by Jon — 'it's not brain surgery.' The little shit." She pulled two steaks off the grill and put them on a nearby platter. "I hope you're hungry. I've been working all day and completely forgot to eat lunch."

"Yes. Is there anything I can do?" She told him to have a seat, and he saw that the patio table and chairs were together as well. "Those I did put together. So be careful when you sit down."

Laughing, he sat. They were sturdy and seemed to be the right size for him. When she came out with her arms full, he took the tray from her and she joined him. He looked at the spread before him and laughed.

"I honestly wasn't hungry until just now. This is amazing." There was salad and baked potatoes, as well as warm bread and all the trimmings for the potatoes, including bacon and sour cream. "I stopped by to see Mom on my way home. She said that you were going to release her tomorrow if she promised to be good. I hope you know that you scared them enough that I think Dad really will tie her down if she tries to get up."

"Good. She lost a great deal of blood. And while I know that she will mend, she's very weak yet and needs to take it easy." They talked about the house that he was working on for Hawkins. "I heard from him today. Well, indirectly. But I got a call from the president."

"He told me he called in some things for you." She nodded. "What did he say? I mean, if you can share."

"The president said that I had been treated poorly by his best men and he wanted to make it up to me. He also asked after you guys and your mom. I gave him as much as I could, and he seemed happy with her results. I'm going to receive my back pay as well as a perk. I'm not sure I deserve something like that, but I have to go to him to get it." Dustin watched her face. After all that had happened, he didn't want her to be upset by it. "Did you know that Hawk put me in for the Medal of Bravery? That I'd gone above and beyond, in his words, to make the men and woman over there go home when all seemed lost?"

He didn't say anything, still trying to gauge her mood around all this. After she finished her dinner and leaned back in her seat, he grabbed the last of the bread and did the same. It was a beautiful evening, with the sun just going down behind the mountain behind them.

"I talked to Boyd today. I know that most of your family already knew I was joining him, but we sat down and discussed what we expected of each other. I'll do most of the operations that we might need, and he'll show me how to be a country doctor." She grinned and closed her eyes. "I've been in a hospital setting nearly my entire career, including the service, and I think I might like this better."

"He loves it. Boyd said that he loves seeing the same family for illnesses. Bringing children into the world, as well as helping them go from this life to the one on the other side." She said that was the hardest for her, death. "I would imagine it would be. You've seen so much of it."

"Yes, I have." She looked out over the field again and he turned to look. "Jon is out there. I don't know why I know that. When he left here earlier he walked away, but he can become anything. I have seen it. He's such a wonderful young man."

"He is. And a good friend too. Jon would never harm you; you do know that, don't you?" She nodded, still looking out over the field. "Mackenzie, what is it? What's wrong?"

~~~

To answer him would tell him her innermost feelings. But she loved him and knew that if anyone could help her, he could do it. She picked up the last bit of brie on her plate and held it between her two fingers.

"My whole life has been pretty much like this cheese. Smooth on the outside. Dry when things were rough. Things were crumbled away from me...my mom, my grandparents, and even my pet." She broke off pieces of it, tiny little bits of cheese that fell to the deck. "I joined the Army right after med school. My thought was, I'd be able to conform to the rules. I didn't have many that made sense to me as a kid, and once I was in, I realized there were some that made less sense than my husband did. Not to say I didn't love him, or at least I thought I did. But I know now it wasn't real. This, with you, is."

"We're going to get him, honey." She knew that too. Again, she was not sure why, but she knew that if anyone could, this family would do their best to bring him down. "Go on, tell me."

"When I got out — it didn't matter how I got out — but once I was out of the service, I wandered around for a little while. I didn't have any sort of commitments. My brother, of course, but he was getting disability and that paid for his care. When I'd go see him, it would make me happy for a while, then sad when I thought of all the things he was missing. Yes, he was violent at times, but as I told you, it was no fault of his own." She put the cheese on the plate and picked up the tomato. "My husband tried his best to break me. Demanding drugs from me. Prescriptions that would supply him with money.

At the time, I had some. A great deal by some standards, but he stole my prescription pad and forged my name on a lot of meds. I nearly lost my license. That was when he cooked up his death, to avoid going to prison, I think. All my money went to court costs and legal fees. And there were plenty of those."

"I would imagine." She nodded and put the tomato down. "What else? What haven't you told me yet?"

"One night, about seven months ago, I was coming home from work. It had been a hell of a day; most of the other doctors had left when their shift ended. I was walking to my car when I was attacked." She smashed the tomato. "It broke me. And it might have killed me but for a vampire that came to save me."

"Victoria." She nodded. "You said that you knew her and that was how. I wondered about that. Go on."

"She took me to her lair and healed me. In exchange, though she didn't ask me for it, I would help her." Mac looked at Dustin then. "Not with blood or money, but with knowledge; well, sort of, but not from the hospital. I would have a victim come in, one that had been killed by either drugs, drive-bys, or gang activity, and she would find the ones who'd done it."

"She'd feed from them. More than likely killing them." Mac nodded. "Do you expect me to be pissed at you for this? To think less of you for it?"

"Yes." He took her hand into his. "You should be. I did everything I was trained not to do to kill. I would do it again too, if I could."

"Good." She asked him if he understood what she had done. "Yes. Completely. You helped Victoria live. You got some scum off the streets, and you were loyal to your job. Saving lives."

"I had those people killed. I'm not supposed to kill. I'm supposed to heal." He said that in his way of thinking, she had. "No, Dustin, I sent her there, knowing full well that she was going to kill them."

"I told you he'd not care a whit." Mac looked at Victoria as she appeared in the seat across from them. "Hello, Dustin. You have yourself a wonderful mate here. I knew that when I first met up with her."

"She is a hell of a woman, yes, I'll agree with you there." She growled at them both, which of course made them laugh. "You are pretty good at that, but you can't beat someone that does it as a cat. It has to come from the belly. Like this."

The growl was spectacular. She watched him for several seconds, then was amazed when he shifted to his large cat. It took her a moment to realize that he wasn't being cute, but that something had startled him. Standing up when Victoria did, they all stared at the tree line that she'd been watching before.

"Something out there?" Victoria nodded. "Something or someone? The reason I ask is, do I need to go and get my kit or run for cover?"

"I can't tell yet. Just don't move." Mac said that she wasn't. "They're coming toward us, but slowly. I can smell blood, but it's tainted. I don't know with what."

"Okay."

The large hawk landed on the deck, then shifted. She wasn't sure what to think when Jon told them to stand down, that it wasn't a threat. No one seemed to heed his words, so she didn't either. Whatever was out there was going to be dead if they didn't show themselves soon.

"It's a captive. Like I was. Hold on, please don't hurt him." Jon put his hand on Dustin and curled his fingers into his fur. "He's someone like me. Not entirely, but he's been out there for some time. He's hurt."

"Can I help him?" Jon said no, he had to heal himself. After he was fed. "I see. And will he be feeding on one of us? I'd like to know…you know, just in case."

Jon turned and looked at her. His smile was brilliant. She found herself grinning back at him. He hugged her to him and she realized how strong he was.

"You have a very vivid imagination. Scary too. No, he doesn't have any desire to feed on or eat you. He's hurt and in need of food, like you would eat. Do you have any vegetables? Fresh is better for him." She told him there was salad left, as well as a bag of carrots and celery. "If you would be so kind as to get that for him, he'll be just fine."

Going into the house, her imagination went off. Was it a giant rabbit? Did he have large teeth like one? All sorts of thing flew around in her head. So much so that when someone touched her shoulder, she screamed and lashed out. Knocking Hawkins to the floor had her helping him up.

"What the fuck is wrong with you? Don't you know that I could have hurt you?" He told her that she had. "What if I had had a gun or something? You'd not think it was so funny then, would you?"

"I didn't want to startle you. You were having a nice conversation with yourself, and I wanted to see what you were talking about." She told him about the person or whatever in the yard. "He's a person."

"How do you…? You know what, I don't care how you

know. What are you doing here, anyway? I thought you'd be out terrorizing someone." She slapped her hand over her mouth when she thought about what she'd said. "I'm so sorry. I never meant to say that. I was scared and you startled me."

"It's fine, Mac. I swear. It's completely my fault. And I came home for a couple of days because I need your help." He pulled his shirt up and she hissed at the wound there. "I pulled the knife out, but there is a piece of it still inside of me. I was wondering if you could see if you could get it out for me. I don't want my family to worry until it's done."

"I have to take some carrots out for.... Just don't move. I'll be back." Taking the food out to the deck, she met the young man. He was young too, about fourteen or fifteen. When he sat in the chair, she could see what it had cost him to come to them. He was in bad shape.

After making sure that he was going to be all right, she went to see her other patient. Hawkins had taken off his shirt and laid out the knife that he'd pulled from himself. She picked it up and saw how much blade she was looking for.

"I'm going to be busy all the time with you around, aren't I?" He told her that perhaps it was fate that brought her to them. "Maybe. But before I begin, I'd like to tell you thanks. You might have saved my life by making me see that being in the service wasn't for me."

"You were close." She nodded and asked him if he wanted anything for pain. "No, it won't work for me. Not unless you have an endless supply of it."

It took her twenty minutes of prodding to get the two pieces out of his side, and then another ten for her to get him to rest. The man was big and heavy, she realized as she helped him to one of the bedrooms. At this rate, she was going to have to open her own place at home to take care of the wounded. Going to the deck, she was surprised to find the young man healed and smiling.

"I'm going to help him get to someone safe. He'll be fine now." She asked him if the family was close by. "No. It's dangerous to have two of us together. I think we send off some sort of signal when we're grouped, and we'll be safer if he is elsewhere."

"Just so long as he's safe, then I can live with that." Jon nodded and asked her if she was all right. "Yes, I guess. I have something going on."

"I understand." She had a feeling that he did too. Going back into the house, she sat with the rest of them and wondered about her newest patient. Hawk wasn't well, even she could see that.

Chapter 8

Hawk opened his eyes but didn't move. His hand was wrapped around his gun, so if there was someone in the room with him that would cause him harm, he was ready. Looking to his right, he saw his dad sleeping, and Mom was on the other side of the bed, knitting. He was glad to see that she was all right, but he wasn't going to ask her. She looked upset to him.

"I do hope you know that you scared ten years off my life. Mackenzie tried to tell us it was nothing, but I know better. You're my son and I know you were in pain." He sat up a little, ignoring the pain for now. "I have it on good authority that you're to take two weeks off. And I plan to make you, too."

"You spoke to my boss?" She nodded and put down her knitting. "You do know that old ladies knit, don't you? And you are far from that."

"I'm having grandchildren by my other sons. And here you lie bleeding from a wound that you more than likely won't tell me how you got." He told her he was sorry. "I don't want you to be sorry, Hawkins, I want you to be safe. How much longer are you going to be doing this?"

"I'm getting out." She looked as shocked as he'd ever seen her. "Something came up and I'm leaving the service. At least as it pertains to me being out in the open all the time. I'll have my twenty in two years from now, and I've made a bargain with the president to work those here from the States. He wants me to train some of the Secret Service on how to do their job." Not all true, but he didn't want to tell her that just yet.

"Does Lauren know?" He said not yet. He'd only just talked to the president yesterday. "Two days ago. You've been resting here for two days. Mackenzie said that you needed it, as she'd not given you anything to combat the pain."

"I'd been working for five days when I got hurt. I was exhausted and not paying my usual attention. It was then that I realized that I'd had enough." His mom moved closer to the bed and took his hand. "I have missed so much being away. And when I spoke to Dustin the other day, about the house that I ended up buying, I realized that it was exactly what I wanted. A home, like the one that you and Dad had for us. Family nearby in the event that I need them. And I know that they'd come, too."

"Yes, even far away like you have been, we would have come to you immediately." He kissed her hand and held it while he lay there. For having so much rest, he was still fighting sleep. "Hawkins, you're all right, aren't you?"

"Yes. I'm going to be all right. I'm not saying that It's going to be easy, entering into this phase of my life, but I'm going to give it my best." She told him that she loved him. "I love you as well, Mom. All of my family."

He closed his eyes and felt his body begin to float into sleep. Hawkins knew that he needed it, more than most, but he also knew that he was safe. For the moment anyway. He was home and his family would protect him for a change. Sleep took him under.

When he woke, his guards had changed. Sitting in the big chair was Colin, and his dad was still in the other chair. But this time he was awake and quietly arguing with his brother. Clearing his throat had them both looking at him.

"He's a stubborn butt. You all are, but this one is making me want to pick up something and hit him over the head. Several times, and very hard. Not that I think it would do much good...he's hardheaded too." Hawk asked his dad who he was referring to. "Your brother there. He thinks just because he's gonna come work with us that he should pay for some of the equipment."

"Why shouldn't he?" Colin grinned at Dad. "I'm not saying that I agree with you, Colin. I'm just wondering why Dad thinks you shouldn't."

"Dad needs a new truck." Okay, Hawk could see that. He had noticed the last time he was home that it was rusty and falling apart. "And they could use a bigger air compressor. The one that they have now leaks like a sieve, and it only holds twenty pounds of air."

"I'm guessing that there are bigger ones out there?" Colin nodded. "Can you afford to get these things? What I mean is, why is it you think they need these things? I don't imagine that they can't afford them if they really wanted them."

"Dad drives the company truck and it needs brakes, a new windshield, as well as tires. The ones that he has on there now are showing cord." Hawk looked at his dad as Colin continued. "The thing burns oil like it's its job. The heat is on all the time, including the summer months, and the windows quit working on it about the time I was born."

"It gets me to here and there, don't it?" Hawk cocked a brow at his dad. "Okay, I could use a new truck. Mom rode with me the other day and told me that I should have warned her about the floor falling out. She nearly lost her purse. And it does get a might hot in there in the summer. But the other stuff, we're making due."

"You think that if you had a larger air compressor you could get more work done on the job site?" His dad said that they might, but they didn't know. "I see. So, since you don't know, then it's more than likely a fact that you could. Dad? What is wrong with him helping out?"

Dad leaned back in his seat, but he wasn't relaxed about it. He hated to lose an argument. And even though no one had lost anything, his dad would still grumble about it. This, Hawk decided, was what he had missed more than anything, and he fell back to sleep.

The next time he woke, he was thankfully alone in the room. Sitting up caused him a little pain, but nothing like he'd had before he came home. Staggering to the bathroom, he turned on the water, and while it was heating up the room, he looked at himself in the mirror.

"You are one ugly fucker." He wiped at the beard that he'd grown while he'd been out. Deciding to shave once he finished his shower, he pulled the gauze off and gingerly touched the wound.

The pain was nearly gone, but the bruise wasn't. He stepped into the water and let the heat of it wash over him.

Then, as carefully as he could, he washed himself and the wound. It wasn't the only place on him that was sore, so he had to be careful not to open other wounds that had scabbed over. After finishing up, he wrapped a towel around his waist and stepped to the sink. By the time he was finished scraping the bristled beard off his face, he was exhausted. After brushing his teeth, he walked into the bedroom. His gun was on the lap of a man sitting in the chair.

"You do know that that is loaded, right? And that the bullets in it are silver and deadly to anyone?" Jarvis Wingate, President of the United States, nodded. "Just so long as you don't shoot off something important. What are you doing here?"

"Lauren called me the first day, but it took me a bit to sneak out. Said you were here and recuperating. How are you feeling?" He showed him the wound. "You haven't shifted yet, I take it."

"Just woke up. What day of the week is this?" Jarvis laughed and told him. "Okay, it seems I've been here for about six days. How many have you been here?"

"I arrived late last night. Much to the exasperation of your newest sister-in-law. I have to tell you, she's a little scarier than Lauren. And she didn't stand on ceremony. Tore right into me about giving her notice and such. She is a hellcat, isn't she?" He said that he hadn't been on the best of terms with her yet. "Yes, she told me. Also told me that whatever you told me wasn't nearly as horrific as you made it out to be when the two of you had your encounter. She's still getting paid, by the way, and her pension has been reinstated. Did you know that she gave that up when she left? Or I should say, she was forced to give it up as a punishment. It's taken care of, as I said."

"Figured as much. And her loans? What about those?" Jarvis said they'd been taken care of as well. "Thank you. I don't think she's going to be any happier when she figures that out."

"I'll leave that to you." Hawk sat down on the bed, ready to lay down and take another nap. "Does your family know the whole story, Hawkins? Or even why you're here and not in the field?"

He knew that he was concerned about him. Hell, he was too. But to be called by his first name and not Hawk or McCullough made him wince a little. Hawk shook his head.

"They know only as little as I could tell them. And that is still more than they needed to know. I did tell them that I was getting out and working for you." Jarvis nodded. "Just so you know, I think that Jon knows, and maybe Mac. I've been here for several days now, and I'm sure she figured something was up. Probably knows more about this than even you and I do. She's that good."

"No doubt she does. I'm impressed with her too. She's done some outstanding things in the few weeks since joining this family. But about you...to have someone poison you, one of your own men, is terrifying. You're very lucky that someone found your body when they did. Had they not.... Well, that's not a phone call I ever want to make to your family. I don't think I could do it." Hawk nodded. "What now?"

"I take the rest of my medical and then I go to work for you." He told him that was not what he meant and he knew it. "What happens to my life now? I mean, you know as well as I that I don't have much longer to live. The doc said six months to a year."

112

"Yes, I know that. It breaks me to know that too. I owe you and your family so much." He nodded, not really wanting to think about his shortened life right now. "When are you going to tell them?"

"Tonight. If I can stay awake long enough." Jarvis stood up. "You sticking around? Or you running off to that cushy job of yours?"

"Cushy? I think not. I'm still cleaning up the mess from my predecessor. You know as well as I do that he left more undone than he ever did to help the country. Anyway, I should get back. Sneaking out is hard enough without pissing people off." Jarvis put out his hand to shake. "If you need me, all you have to do is call. And everything that you asked for, it's taken care of as well."

"Thanks."

When he was alone, he continued to sit on the bed. He wasn't feeling any better, but good enough to shift. However, he wasn't ready for that yet. Soon, he promised himself.

He was going to die. There was something so final about that. Hawk had worked in the most dangerous places in the world, doing jobs that no one he knew would want to do, and hadn't been anything more than hurt. Now, because he'd been in the wrong place at the wrong time, he'd contracted a deadly poison. And had it not been for the fact that he was a shifter, he would have died there instead of coming home to deal with it.

~~~

Mac wasn't sure how to talk to the big man. He'd come down the stairs not an hour ago, and had been dozing off and on since then. Sitting in the chair across from him, she waited for him to open his eyes again before she spoke.

"I ran tests." He said he'd figured she would. "Does anyone else know? I mean, other than the person that hit you with that?"

"The president. You and me." He asked her who she'd told. Before she could reply, he answered himself. "If you had told anyone, they would be here now. So, I'm assuming that you've kept it to yourself."

"I didn't even tell Dustin." He nodded and sat up on the couch a little higher. "I can fix you. I mean, I can make it so it doesn't kill you. I know how."

"No, they said it was in my bloodstream and that I won't be able to even get a transfusion to take care of it." Mac handed him the journal that she'd found for him. It had a part of her work in it. "What's this?"

"I was where you were, remember? I know what you were given and how to combat it. This article, I wrote it when my research was only in the infant stages. I have it figured out now." Hawk studied her, but said nothing. "You can't work for several weeks after I'm done. I mean, you could, but it would be harder on you than the drug currently is on your body. I can start as soon as you tell your family. I'll need them. All of them."

"Why?" Mac got up to pace and she knew that he was watching her. "Is this payback for what I did to you over there?"

She hadn't meant to slap him. It hadn't been in her mind to cause him any more pain than he was in now, but as soon as she did it, he told her how sorry he was. And that he knew better.

"I should hope so. I need you to tell your family because they have the blood that I need should Jon's blood not do the trick. It takes a village to raise a child, and a family to hold it together. I heard that when I was working on this project, and I think it's fitting. A transfusion won't work, as you know. I'll need to completely drain your body of all your blood and force fresh blood, your family's blood, into you. And that of a few others, like Jon and Victoria. Who both know, by the way. I didn't tell them; Jon knew and Victoria was here when I took your blood to run a few tests. She...well, she told me that she smelled it."

"And this force of family blood, how does it work?" She didn't want to tell him, but knew that if he didn't have all the details, he'd not do it. What she was hoping for was that Jon would be able to save the day so that this secondary plan didn't have to be put into place. "Mac? What is it you're trying very hard not to say?"

"Everyone will be weak, of course. Giving blood will do that to anyone, but when you're getting this done, you'll basically be dead. Your heart will stop beating, because I'm going to make sure that it does, but your brain will be fine. There is a slight possibility that you might have some side effects." He asked her what sort. "Well, I don't know what the vampire blood or Jon's will do to you. So I sort of...I took some of his and it affected me."

"How?" Stopping her pacing, she put out her hands and let them shift, just her hands, into different animals. "You can do that to your whole body?"

"Yes, just as Jon and Reese can." He nodded and sat up more. "You'd have a good deal more of their blood so...I was thinking that I could just use a bit of Jon's first to see if that would do the trick, but that would be up to you. He's scary powerful, and so is his blood. But as I said, that would be

115

entirely up to you."

"And how does this work?" She explained to him about the equipment that she'd use and how it worked. But told him that she'd only tasted Jon's blood and it had worked this well. "When can we do this? And how long does it take?"

"You mean just using Jon's or all of it?" He told her Jon's. "An hour. Maybe less...I don't know for sure on that. How much you'll need is the variable too. You're a lot bigger than I am. And your muscle mass should be considered as well. There are just too many variables to tell you how much or how long for a certainty."

She paced again. There was so much that could go wrong, and it might not even work on him. He was not only a bit bigger than her test subject had been, but he was also a shifter. Mac told him that as she moved back and forth across the room.

"And why is it that I need to tell my family? I mean, other than I might need their blood if this doesn't work?" She told him. "So you think that if I shouldn't come out of this, that they'll blame you. They won't. Not any of them. But I'll tell them. I was going to tell them anyway. I like this better, because there might be a better outcome thanks to you. Something more positive to look forward to than my impending death."

"Thank you." He nodded and asked if he could talk to her. "Yes, but if it's about what happened over there, I don't want to talk about it."

"But I do. I need to tell you how sorry I am. And ask that you forgive me for being such an asshole. I'm not usually like that." She only stared at him. "Okay, I am like that all the time, but not to women. Not usually."

Mac sat down. She supposed now was as good a time as

any to clear the air. And as much as she didn't want to think about it, she knew there was a chance that he might not make it. Mac knew that her not telling him that she had forgiven him might haunt her for the rest of her life.

"I've talked to his mom." He told her that he knew that. "She had always expected that one day she'd be the one to see him like that. Mary told me that is why she never reads the information that comes on the crates. She doesn't want to know if it's someone else's son that she might know."

"She told me that too. That she doesn't want to know a name any more than she wanted to find her son like that. But she said, to have made you do what I wanted you to do would have been even harder on her." Mac asked why. "She said that the way he came to her was what had happened and it finalized his death. To have seen him like he'd only gone for a nap, it would have been difficult for her to comprehend. This way, she said, while hard, was how he died. Not a pretty version, but real."

"Had I known, or had an idea that.... Well, I'm not sure that I would have done it then either. There were others that needed me, and helping him wasn't going to keep them alive." Hawk said he knew that now. "I'm sorry. About everything."

"As am I. What I did was wrong. And if you could forgive me, I'd honestly sleep better at night." She put out her hand and he took it, making her feel better than she had in years. "You and I are going to be good friends, I know it, Mackenzie McCullough."

Leaving him after talking for another hour, she set things up. Hawk was going to ask to have dinner with his family, and she set that up too. She was just coming out of the kitchen when Dustin came in. He kissed her soundly and she told him that she loved him.

"I have to talk to you about something. We're having dinner at your parents' house too. That's where Hawk will tell you what is going on." He kissed her again. "I love you. With all that I am."

"I love you too. Now, are you willing to tell me what is going on?" She did. All of it. "Well, for all the things I thought you were going to say, that wasn't even close to it."

"I'm sorry. I couldn't tell you and break his confidence in me." Dustin said that he understood. "He is going to talk to your family tonight. And tell them what we're going to do to try and fix this."

"Mom is going to have a cow. Not at you, but because he didn't tell her right off." Mac said she understood that. "And my dad.... He's not going to take it well either. Just to let you know. For all his toughness, he's a big old kitten. I fell when I was about ten and broke my leg. He cried for an hour. And it wasn't even that bad."

"He loves you. Your entire family loves with all that they have. I think that's why I love them too." She let him hold her as she finished what she was going to do. Jon was going to be playing a huge role in this, and she hoped that his parents would be all right with it. "Are you kidding? I think they'd lay down their life for Hawkins. Jon is just a boy, yes, but even if they didn't want him to do it, he'd feel it was his duty to do so. He loves his new family."

"Still, I want him to get their permission for this. I don't want anyone backing out at the last minute. It could mean Hawk's life." Dustin said that he'd make sure they were all onboard, and if not, then she'd know who wasn't going to. "I don't think anyone will say no, but we have to make sure."

"You're right. And we'll figure it out." Hawkins joined them in the dining room and Dustin hugged his older brother. "I love you, man."

They held each other for several minutes, neither of them saying anything. Mac felt her eyes fill with tears; it was such a wonderful sight to see love like this, especially between brothers. When they were finished, Hawk pulled her into his arms and held her too. Tears fell down her cheeks when he told her that he loved her too.

Moving away from them, she told them she had to go and see her own brother. Erwin was asking for her. Going out to the car, she had to sit for several minutes to gather her thoughts. Love. She'd never in all her life remembered having such profound love for someone. She loved her brother, yes, but not as this family did one another. She was looking forward to many years with this family and their togetherness.

The jail where he had been taken had transferred him to another place, one that was better prepared to take care of his needs. She headed there now, hoping that this time when she saw him, he'd be able to tell her what Walton had said to him. Stopping by the store first, she picked him up some magazines, as well as some treats. Erwin loved trail mix with the tiny candies in it.

Pulling up in front of the place, she smiled at the setting. It looked like something from a fairy tale. Gingerbread working around the eves, flowers along the gate, and a sidewalk leading to the door, with a welcome sign on the front door. She could also see a garden in the back and several people working in it. One of them was her brother.

Chapter 9

Walton wasn't in the best of humor. Of course, he never was of late, especially since someone had moved his idiot brother-in-law and his ex-wife was not cooperating. Well, if he could find her, he knew that he could convince her to change her mind. It was either she did that or he'd kill her. Which was more than likely going to happen anyway. He read the front of the newspaper and felt pissed all over again.

"Married? To some fuckwad that is moving in on my territory?" He looked at the picture of the happy couple that had accompanied the article he'd read last night. "Who the fuck does she think she is, marrying? Fucking bitch is gonna have to toe the line better now that she has a new hubby. Especially if she doesn't want me to hurt him too while I'm at it."

He'd found out through the grapevine who she had gotten to marry her. Some construction worker, of all things. She was a doctor, not some idiot that went around fixing up old ladies' houses for a living. Walton wondered if there was even any kind of money in doing that shit. Her new hubby was only hanging onto her coattails, just as Walton had tried to do.

"Not that I'm going to be doing that shit." He thought of all the jobs he'd had over his lifetime. Most of them had been tweeners…ones that gave him pocket money while he was between it and his next big idea. And Walton always had those. The problem was, he never had the money to make them happen.

The drug lord thing had been his biggest and stupidest. But after spending a few weeks being chased by the cops because of Mac, he'd figured that he wasn't going to be able to make that one happen. But the problem was, he'd gotten hooked on them instead of making any sort of profit. Taking Erwin, the retard's, meds had been a happier time for him, but that had been cut off when his wife had gotten it in her head to have Erwin tested. She was forever sticking her nose into places that it didn't belong. And not doing a damned thing to make his life any better.

"Not very loving of you, my dear ex-wife." Walton looked around the shabby room he'd been in for a month now, and wondered why he'd not demanded money when she'd served him with the divorce papers. Of course, being in jail hadn't given him much of an opportunity to fight her on anything. It was a done deal by the time he'd gotten word that she'd been granted a divorce.

Walton had loved Mac. He'd even thought it was nice that she was going to college to better herself. Well, he'd thought it was great until she started working longer hours than he wanted her to, and not helping out around the apartment. And when she did have a day or two off, some of it was spent with Erwin. He currently hated that man more than he did his ex.

"But the money sure was nice." He'd found himself finding more and more things to buy with her money. Getting in and out of schemes had gotten him into trouble, but Mac was always there to bail him out of it. Until he started knocking her around. That hadn't set well with her, and she'd put up a fuss.

So of course, instead of backing off, like he probably should have, he hit her more, knocking her around enough that she'd had to have surgery, as well as some time off work. Having her up his ass all the time hadn't done much for their relationship either. And he fucked up one too many times for the Army. Getting himself discharged hadn't bothered him that much, but she sure did take it hard. So again, like a fool, he'd hit her hard enough that she'd gotten his ass arrested.

After he'd lost his source of ready cash and his drug of choice from the retard, he had had to get it somehow. That was when he'd come up with the idea that she could — and should, with her being his wife — give them to him. She'd objected to that too, the damned goody-two-shoes. Then he had found his ass in big trouble and had to do something. Killing himself seemed, to him, at least, the most logical step.

That had been a brilliant idea. It had worked like a charm. And he'd been able to collect on an insurance policy that had given him enough money to pursue other dreams. Also to get all the happy shit he wanted. Even coming up with his mom as the beneficiary had gone better than he'd ever hoped for. He'd been free of the police, his ex-wife was right where he wanted her to be, and he had some cash. The Internet had been very helpful in getting his scheme into working order.

And telling him how not to get caught.

But then other things started to mess up his life. The drugs hadn't been easy to find that were cheap enough for him to afford. The money that he'd always taken when he wanted was gone now, and the insurance payoff hadn't gone nearly as far as he thought it should. Mac hadn't been an easy touch either. She wouldn't even pony any over to him when he found her alone. Hiring guys to beat her to shit had dried up too, especially when they found out that she was with her new family. The McCulloughs were some kind of big deal to people, he'd figured out.

Walton hadn't been a terrible husband. He knew this. The fact that he had knocked her around a few times shouldn't have been counted against him. He'd only done it to keep her in line. He knew a lot of other men who had put their wives in the hospital almost weekly. The Army had frowned on it, but so long as she didn't go to the hospital too much, he was getting by with it.

The few times, four or five at the most, hadn't been all that bad. And when he'd tried to tell her that, explain how he was a better husband than most, she'd gone off and had him booted out of the service, then later into prison.

He surfed the stations on the television and found his show. When he'd been in jail all that time, they'd put it on the television during the day, and as hard as he'd tried not to get all caught up in their stupid lives, he'd found himself hooked. Walton watched it while looking through the books he'd found in the room...a Bible and a smut book that his mom used to read all the time. Tossing them across the room, he watched the soap opera until a commercial came on.

Walton didn't have a cell phone. He did at one time, but

that too had been because he'd been married to a rich doctor. He'd been stupid to have used her script pad that one time, and had nearly gotten her fired. An unemployed wife was one that didn't have any income. He should have been smarter and stolen someone else's. Not that anyone ever checked for that shit, but he'd fucked up. So when the phone beside the bed started ringing, he nearly didn't answer it. Picking it up, he was careful not to speak until they did.

"Mr. Thomas, I presume." He felt his skin crawl when the woman laughed. "This is Victoria. I'm a friend of your ex-wife's. I was wondering if I could persuade you to just go fuck yourself. And barring that, you know, die. Stepping in front of a truck or bus, or even jumping off a bridge. Either one would suit me."

"Who the fuck is this?" She sighed heavily. "You can't be telling me that you want me to die. That isn't right."

"Isn't it? Oh well, then let me be more point blank. You will die if you go near Mackenzie or any other McCullough again. And that would include Erwin. Does that suit your needs better? I would hope that you'd save me the trouble of having to kill you myself, but I don't think you're going to be that nice, are you?" He asked her again who she was. "Are you a simpleton? I have told you my name. Listen to me hard this time. I. Am. Victoria."

"Well, Vicki, why don't you bring yourself on over here and let me show you why you're not going to kill me? I have myself a nice gun here that I'm just itching to try out on someone." She told him it was daylight. "So? You so ugly that you can only be out in the dark where people don't see you? All right, we'll have us a good old time, you and me."

"I'm sure you'd like to think that, but—and this is from

125

a great many admirers and now my mate—I'm not ugly at all. I'm a vampire." He started to laugh, figuring that she'd join him soon enough. But all she did was tell him how old she was. "So, as you can well imagine, I've got a great deal of magic that I'm just...what did you call it? Oh yes, I'm just itching to use on you."

He scratched his arm, then his palm. "I don't believe in vampires. What kind of shit are you trying to pull on me?"

"Shit? None. But I don't give a fuck who or what you believe in. By the way, do you itch, Walton? Do you have a nasty rash on your dick that makes you want to scratch it hard enough to draw blood? How about those little berries of yours? Do you feel the burn?"

He had to remove his pants and underwear to get to his privates. Christ, it was like he'd been laying in a bed of poison ivy. His dick hurt so bad that he thought a cold bath would help. When he laid the phone back in the cradle, he heard her laughing. Whatever she'd done to him—and he had no doubt that she'd done it—he was on fire.

By the time he was soaking in a cool bath of water, he had bloodied himself. His dick now looked like he'd taken a rake to it, and his balls were so swollen that he couldn't even touch them with a towel. And the towels in this hotel were the softest things he'd ever felt.

He needed some ice. Icing down his balls was the only thing he could think to do to bring the pain down. But going down to the ice machine with a bucket meant he had to pull on some pants, and even not wearing underwear, they were going to make him cry. So there he lay in the cold water. Walton didn't have any idea what he was going to do now.

Victoria had said that she was a friend of Mac's. That

meant that she'd had something to do with this. He still wasn't sure how he'd been hurt like he was, but he was sure that these two women were the root of all his pain.

"I'm going to make them both pay." He thought of her telling him she was a vampire. "Bullshit."

He believed there were other creatures around. He'd seen a wolf once that he was sure was one of them night creatures. Anything that wasn't human, everyone knew, could only come out at night. Then once, when he'd been fucking some broad, he was sure that she'd changed when she came. Crying out in some other language that had his cock and balls shrivel up.

He looked down at himself. Christ, he'd done a number on himself. His poor old cock was bloodied raw, like he'd been fucking a rosebush. And his balls looked like they'd been used as a punching bag, they were so big and painful.

Cooling off the water again, he thought about Mac and what he was going to have her do for him. He was done with the drug thing. He just wanted money now. And some cream. Of course he was going to knock her around some more. Maybe even kill her. She'd done about all she could for him, and now that he was itching like…. He'd been scratching again, and now his water was pink with blood. He was going to have to do something or he'd end up scratching his dick right off.

~~~

Rich helped with the hoeing. He'd never in all his days seen anybody so excited about putting a few seeds in the ground. When he heard his name, he looked up and saw Mackenzie coming toward him and Erwin.

"Hey there, pretty lady. My goodness, you're a sight for

127

sore eyes. This here young man is about to wear me down."
He watched Erwin as he'd been told to do so that he didn't
hurt anyone. So far all he'd done was bite on the side of his
hand and tell him that he liked carrots. "Erwin and I are going
to have us some nice fat potatoes sometime."

"Carrots." He nodded at him and put the hoe back in the
big bucket that had been brought out for them all to use. "I
like carrots. They're for rabbits."

"You been here long?" He told Mackenzie that he'd only
been there about an hour. "I didn't know that any of you guys
were aware that he was here. This is my third visit. And I
think it's wonderful how Erwin loves it here."

She was feeling guilty. So Rich put her at ease with it,
telling her that he'd only been told because he was a friend
of the couple that owned the place. He didn't tell her that
him and Bea were part owners; he was thinking that she'd be
thinking all kinds of things about that. Mac was a bit skittish
about things.

"Can I have a hug?" Erwin squealed at her request, but
he was very careful when he did hug her. In his excitement
earlier, Erwin had knocked him down. He'd forgotten, or
maybe didn't realize, that he was so much bigger than the
others who shared this home with him. "You are having fun
with Mr. McCullough?"

"Grandpa. He said I could call him Grandpa. He's not,
you know?" Mackenzie said that she did. "You gonna stay
until the carrots come up? I had two of them this morning. I
like them a whole lot, Sissy."

"You did?" Rich started to tell her that they planted the
carrot seeds, then the staff came out to put fresh carrots in the
ground for the residents. They ate them better, he'd been told.

But he had a feeling that she knew that already. "How about I come back tomorrow and we can have some for breakfast again? I really liked them the other day when we had them for lunch, didn't you?"

"Yes, okay." He wandered off from her and Rich watched Mac. She was sad, he knew that, but he was sure it was more than just seeing her brother.

"When I was about six he came into my room to have me read him a story. I knew from the start that he was different than other big brothers, but I loved him anyway. After that first night, he'd come in all the time and I'd teach him whatever I had learned in school that day. Even as old as he was, it was like he and I were on the same level." Rich told her that he could read well. "Yes. It was easy to teach him, he was so willing to learn. It's the little things that he forgets. Like dressing. Brushing his hair and teeth. And having him remember not to use the same brush for both."

Rich laughed. He wasn't sure that she'd meant it to be funny, but it had caught him off guard. Telling her he was sorry, she told him it was all right. She had thought it was funny too.

"He's not on the same level as some of these adults. Thanks to you, I'm betting. Where are your parents?" She told him. "I'm sorry about that. To lose one is hard enough, but to have them both die in a senseless accident is terrible."

"I suppose. I mean, they were our parents, but they weren't all that affectionate. Not like you guys are. It wouldn't have occurred to them to have given a hug, and even an encouraging word from them would have taken too much time out of their social lives. There wasn't any money, not really, but they had a good time with what they had." He told her again that he was sorry. "It's all right. I'm glad that you're here. I wanted to talk to you about Hawk."

"He told his momma and me. Whatever you need, you let us know and we'll make sure that you have it. And my boys, they've all chimed in that they'll be there to help out too." He took his big blue hankie out of his pocket and wiped at his nose. Rich had been crying off and on for the last hour, just thinking about his sons. "They mean the world to me. More than my own life. When one of them is sick or hurting like my boy is, it tears into my heart like a knife. I'm sure you feel the same for young Erwin there."

"I'm in love with Dustin." He said he knew that. "He asked me to marry him. Soon, as a matter of fact. I guess someone put it in the paper that we already tied the knot."

"I think that might have been Larson. He said that it might make your ex a little on the stupid side. Well, stupider, I guess you could call it. He's not overly bright, is he?" She mentioned how he'd faked his own death. "Yeah, there is that. But I'm thinking he might have had some help with that. Perhaps he looked it up on the Internet. I'm to understand that there is a lot of useful information out there about anything."

She eyed him. Rich had a feeling that he was being sized up. It made him want to stand taller, push out his chest a little more. But he didn't. He just stood there and let her have her look-see.

"You're not the down to earth, good old boy that you let on to be, are you?" Rich asked her what she meant. "You know, I bet if I was to look into your life, I'd find that not only do you a master's degree in something, but I'm betting you might have a doctorate as well, don't you?"

"I just don't know what you mean." He did though. While

he didn't have the latter, he did have a master's degree in engineering. So did Dustin, as well as in business management. And not once, in all the time he'd been working on houses, had it ever occurred to him to finish up his education. "You won't tell on an old man, will you?"

She laughed. And he'd bet his last nickel that it was something that she wasn't used to. Some people laughed all the time. But not this woman. And he'd also bet that she'd done a lot more of it since she'd been with his son.

Erwin came back to talk to them several times. Mackenzie and he sat on the swing and enjoyed the afternoon. If he'd have been asked, he would say that they'd not said a single thing that was important, yet it made him feel like he'd gotten closer to the younger woman and her brother. When they were ready to leave, Erwin came to hug them both again.

"You'll be coming back, won't you, Sissy?" Mac told him she'd be there in the morning. "I'd like that. I got some tests in the morning too. You can stay and help me with them. It's okay if you do. I know my colors good."

"Well. You know your colors well." He grinned, and all Rich could think was that he was just a little boy in a big man's body. "Erwin, remember what I told you about Walton. He's going to get you into trouble. Remember what I told you."

"You said to go and tell somebody that he's bothering me." He looked at Rich then back at his sister. "He hurts you too, huh?"

"Yes, but I have someone that will help us both. So long as you don't let him take you again. You belong here, no matter what. I can't come to see you if you get into trouble and they put you in that home again." He said he promised to be good. "See that you do. I love you, Erwin, and I don't want anything

131

to happen to you."

"I love you too, Sissy. Don't let him hurt you either. Okay?" She said that she wouldn't. "Grandpa, you'll watch over her, won't you? I can't let her get hurt no more. She's all I got."

"You have me and the rest of us, young man. But having a sister like Mac here, that's the best a person can hope for." Erwin nodded and hugged them both after asking if it was all right. Rich was to his car when he turned to Mackenzie and asked her about that.

"He's terrified of hurting me. Anyone, I suppose. That's what got him into trouble in the first place. Erwin forgets how much bigger he is than most people, and he gets really excited when there are people around him. Not in a bad way, though there are people that believe he wants to hurt them, but he's a good person. Just dealt a crappy hand."

"How did Walton treat him?" He didn't think she was going to answer him, but he was sure that was an answer anyway. Her not wanting to tell told him that Walton needed to have his butt handed to him. "I see. And that didn't help him either, did it?"

"No. When he screamed at him or hit him, Erwin didn't understand that. He can learn some things, as I've said, but when he gets into trouble, like he was with Walton all the time, he forgets to be careful or he gets frustrated and combative. Walter would egg him on and then blame him when it got out of hand. It's one of the reasons that I divorced him. He was never good with my brother. I don't think he realized that we were a package when we wed. And he resented the time that I would want to spend with him. What did he expect me to do, leave him in the care of others while he ignored my love for my brother?" Rich nodded. "Why did you come out here today? You had no reason to visit him. Why?"

"I have a reason to visit him. He's related to you, and I wanted to get to know him." Mackenzie didn't seem convinced. "I wanted to talk to him about Walton, too. I didn't want him to get himself wrapped up with the man again. I'm glad to know that you already did that, but he's family, same as you, and I wanted him to know me too."

"I don't think he'll have anything more to do with him. But Walton was the only male figure in his life for a while, and he doesn't understand why he didn't like him. And that's a big thing for him, for people to like him." Rich said he could understand that. "I think you do. You're a nice man, Rich. Do people tell you that enough?"

"Never." They both laughed. "All right now. We'll get ourselves on home. I got it from my missus that she's ordered in some food for this thing. I know that nobody will feel like eating, so she's laid out some tempting things. And Reese, she's been nervous baking again. Bea said the kitchen smelled like a bakery. All them good smells is gonna tempt all of us, I'm thinking."

"That girl needs a shop. Or something to put her things in. Yesterday I had one of her scones. That's all she said it was, just a scone. My goodness. It was like eating a piece of heaven. So of course, I ate three of them." She laughed again as she got in her car. "If she keeps this up, I might weight four hundred pounds in no time."

Chapter 10

Dustin held his brother's hand. Hawkins was very still while things were explained, but he wasn't fooled by it. He was afraid, just as the rest of them were. But they weren't going to be the one that was going to be taking on what Hawkins was.

"The poison has been slowed down in the process of taking over his body because of what he is. If he'd have been human, or even a weaker shifter, he'd be dead already. Some of the effects of it are already making themselves known to him." Mackenzie explained how he was weaker and had lost his ability to stand up for very long. "As I've said, I don't know what Jon's blood is going to do for him, other than more than likely heal him, but it's better than the alterative."

"I'll say." Dad looked around the room as he continued. "And if this doesn't work, we're going to go with plan B, right?"

"Yes, but plan B will have to wait until we can get him into the other rooms of the house. The equipment is there and set

135

up. Everything is ready." Dustin had been both terrified and happy that Jarvis had made sure that they had whatever they had needed in the event this didn't work. "Are you ready?"

"Yes, but I'd like to say one thing." Mackenzie nodded at Hawkins. "I wanted to tell you again how very sorry I am that I hurt you. And to also tell you that I love you. As much as I do the rest of my family. And if this goes south, then you—"

"No. We're not gonna talk about that." Hawkins tried to speak again, but Dad cut him off. "No. Please. I need to think positive on this. If you don't believe, then how can the rest of us? We're going to say *when* this works because I need to believe this as much as I need my next breath."

They settled down again and Jon came to stand beside the cot that had been set up in the living room. Dustin wasn't sure who had decided that this room was large enough to hold them all, but after the furniture was moved back, he could see that it was. They needed to be close.

"You ready for this?" Hawkins told Jon as ready as he'd ever be. "If you grow boobs or something equally weird, it's because I had a burrito for lunch. If you get to craving something strange, that's not my fault either."

"I won't blame you. However, if I have a kid after this is done, I'm totally having it call you Dad." The humor was stale and dirty, but it did break the tension a little. Hawkins squeezed Dustin's hand and waited for Jon. "Give it to me, buddy."

Jon cut his own wrist, but not deeply. Mackenzie had cautioned him to be careful not to do it too deeply, or too long. They wanted Hawkins to receive the blood slowly, so that in the event something unknown happened, they could stop the flow quickly. Dustin wasn't sure what the unknown could have been. No one seemed to know what was going to happen. However, they were all okay with the unknown on this. Whatever happened, they'd work around it. They were family, after all.

It didn't take long for something to occur. Hawkins had been hooked up to heart and brain monitors. When the beeping started to take on a high whine, Dustin was reminded of when his mom had been hurt. Squeezing his brother's hand tighter, he was glad when he returned the tightness.

Mackenzie kept taking Hawkins' blood pressure, and Boyd was monitoring the machines. It looked like neither of them were upset about the noises that were occurring with this, so he tried his best to relax as well. It wasn't until Mackenzie told Jon to stop for a moment that he realized that she was nervous too.

"Hawk, we're going to draw some blood, but I'd like for you to see if you can shift your hands. I know that you can become a cat, but if you could — I don't know — let your hand become a hawk's talon, like your name would suggest, then we can see if it's working." Hawkins held out his free hand and nothing happened. "Just a little more than — "

"No. Wait. I'm thinking about it. I've never seen a hawk before. Not up close, anyway." Everyone waited, and it wasn't until he had a slight headache that Dustin realized that he wasn't breathing. Hawkins grinned at them all. "Look at that. I'm part bird."

They were good claws. And when he flexed them, Dustin felt the bite from them. Letting his brother go so that he could nurse his wound, he watched in fascination as Hawkins shifted and turned into a great bird of prey. As Hawk was flying around the room, Dustin was shocked when a drop of blood hit the small wound on his hand. Looking at Jon, he thought the younger man winked at him. The wound, a small tear in his flesh, healed immediately. Faster even than if he had done it on his own.

"Come down here this minute." Dad was laughing hard, but trying his best to be stern. When Hawkins landed at his feet, Dad sat down on the floor with him. "How you feeling, son? Better? Worse?" Hawkins shifted from beast to man in seconds, with his clothing on and no apparent wounds.

"I feel fantastic." Boyd asked if he could take a sample of blood. "Yes, please do. But I have to tell you, I've not felt this wonderful in years. Maybe my entire life."

The blood test was going to be quick. Again, thanks to Jarvis, the needed equipment was there for them to see if this had worked or not. It would take time for the results, but all of them could see that things did look good. After his brother shifted into other animals, his body trembling with newfound energy, he said, Mackenzie took the sample.

Jon sat next to him at the table. Dustin had been working on this room for a couple of weeks last summer, putting in new windows, laying hardwood flooring, and new cabinets. Now they wanted to expand more. He was excited to start on this project for them. Jon poked him in the ribs.

"I helped you with Mac." Dustin frowned. "You had to be the same. I didn't want her to be without you."

"I don't understand." Jon took his hand and looked at the small scar there. "You didn't do this. Hawkins did when he was working on shifting."

"Yes, but my blood is in your body as well. It's all it took, a single drop of it, to make Mac into what she is. And that, apparently, is all it takes to give you life." Dustin started to ask him what he was talking about when he looked at Mackenzie. "You and she, you'll live forever now. The same as me. You'll grow older, of course, but you won't die from health issues or old age. Removing your head will kill you, but nothing to your heart. It's safe too."

"You did this to us? Why?" He said that he'd had to, for Mackenzie. "Does she know? I mean, you did tell her that you made her an.... Holy shit, Jon, Hawkins is as well."

"Yes. And so are your parents and mine. The babies were easy to help along. Not the others as yet. I believe that Boyd has figured it out and has been avoiding me, but I'll catch him. But to be honest with you, it wasn't until I gave my blood to Mac that I realized what it would do. Then I've been going about making you all immortal. And in answer to your question, no, Mac does not know. Not yet. I wanted to be sure first that I could catch you."

Dustin tried to think of the implications of being immortal. There were a great deal, too. His parents were...they'd be around forever instead of dying and leaving them. The kids, their children, would.... He asked Jon about that.

"I'm not sure. I mean, if you're asking me about your children, I don't know what they'll get from this. If nothing, then I can help them as well. I'd like to say I have all the answers, but I don't. Like you, I'm just figuring this out." Jon grinned. "There are perks as well as bad things that could happen, Dustin. Like being around forever means that you can see your family grow up. See them have children and on down the line. Not to mention, the knowledge that you can give them. Growing up as an immortal will be easier for them, as they won't ever have to think of dying. And I need you, all of you, here with me."

139

"What will other people say? I mean, the town's people. Won't they notice that we're still hanging around long after everyone around us is dead?" Jon said he was borrowing trouble. Vampires did it all the time. "This is a lot to take in... you know that, don't you?"

"Yes. But your brother is going to be fine. You all will live for a very long time, and I won't ever have to be alone. Neither will you." He looked over at Hawkins as he held one of Colin's children. "He will have his own someday. And his will have the blood that he has. I gave him much more than I did even Mac. And when his mate comes, she will be special too."

"How do you know?" When he didn't get an answer, he looked at his nephew. "Jon, what do you know about his mate? Is she here now?"

"No, but she is coming. Not soon. She has her own set of problems. And when she gets here, there will be a time when you will thank me for what I have done for you." Dustin thanked him for what he'd done now. "You're very welcome. But there is trouble coming. Today, as a matter of fact. Walton, he will come to your home, and you must let Mac deal with him. No matter your frame of mind."

"Will she be hurt?" He nodded, but said she'd not be killed. "I don't want her hurt. I want her healthy and happy."

"Happiness will come to her. But a little pain for it isn't so bad. She needs to deal with him on her own terms. Confidence is a terrible thing to lose." Dustin knew that, but he was still nervous about this. "Trust me when I tell you, Dustin, she will be a much better mate when this is done. She needs to finish this with Walton or it will linger in her mind for decades."

"I trust you. Right now I'm not sure what to think about

this, but I do trust you." He watched Mac as she played with one of the twins. "She's happy now. I've never seen her so happy."

"She is in love. With you." Dustin felt the words settle in his heart. Yes, he'd told her that he loved her and she him, but to hear someone else say it, to have it out there, it made him feel as if he could handle anything. And anyone. "The results are in."

The timer buzzed when Jon spoke. He didn't ask him; Dustin had a feeling that not only had it worked, but that Mackenzie was going to tell them about the additive that she'd located in Hawkins' blood. When she came back in the room she was dancing, and that alone told them all that it had been a success. The rest? Well, he'd deal with it when it came.

~~~

Walton could barely breathe around the pain. His dick was so swollen that it looked like he had a permanent erection. But the thought of touching himself, or even to have someone else do it, made him ill. And he'd not peed since the day before yesterday. He was going to die if he didn't get help soon. Making his way to where he knew Mac was living, he held his gun tightly in his hand, knowing that if he let it go, he was going to gouge at himself again. Bending over, even to tie his shoes, had nearly had him putting his gun in his mouth and ending his miserable life.

"Fucking bitch is going to help me or die. But first I'm gonna make her suffer like I have been." He walked like a man with a pole up his ass. The towel around his waist, the only thing that he could remotely stand to touch him, was soaked through with blood. And walking had him sobbing with pain.

141

Yesterday he'd gotten up screaming. His balls were seeping now…he'd scratched them so much that he was sure that he was going to lose them. And his fingers were raw. The way he'd been using them on himself had hurt him in more ways than he could have ever imagined. Mac was going to pay for this fucking shit she'd done to him.

Walton wasn't entirely clear on how she was to blame. His mind was a jumble of thoughts, his body hurting too much, everywhere now, to have a single thought pause long enough for him to think on it. When he'd been in the bathtub again, where he spent most of his time — that or standing in front of the air conditioner unit with his dick gently in his hand — he thought of the phone call.

"She did something to me. That vampire." He didn't believe in them any more than he had before, but there was something about her. She had some kind of magic to make him do this to himself. As he walked, his legs wide apart so that he didn't touch himself, he thought of the first thing he was going to make her do.

"Her?" He had also begun talking to himself. Confusion was making him do all kinds of things he'd not ever done before. "Which her are you speaking about?"

That was another thing. Even though he'd never seen this supposed vampire, he could actually see her face. A beautiful woman with large breasts and pouty lips. He had not a single clue why she invaded his thoughts and dreams, but he could see her as clearly as he could Mac. There were times when he thought of that woman, either of them, that they'd blend into one person. Mac's hair with the pouty lips. Big breasted vampire with Mac's eyes. Stopping to rest again, he leaned heavily against the building he was near.

142

Walton thought about the vampire...Victoria, she'd told him, was her name. When he went to see Mac, he was sure she was going to be there, and she'd kill him for not doing what she had told him to do and, stay away from the McCulloughs. At this point, he was pretty sure that he'd let her. But Mac, she'd fix him up and he'd be as good as new. Or he hoped so. Moving again, he thought of all the ways he was going to make the bitch pay. Either of them.

"Mac is going to make me better or I'll kill that husband of hers. I will anyway, but I can hold him while she does her thing. Being a doctor, she won't be able to not help me, right?" His mind answered yes, that was right. "I need something for pain too. No more fucking around with being a drug lord. I need something fucking good too. I hurt."

The tears fell down his cheeks and he wiped at them, careful of his fingers. He sobbed a little more then, holding his gun tightly to his chest as he mumbled about the pain and aggravation of this shit. Walton was a mess. More than that, he was a horrible mess, and it wasn't his fault.

"I'd been a good husband to her. I only hit her when she needed it." Shouldn't have done that, his mind told him. "But I loved it. I mean, my own daddy hit my mom and she took it. And for weeks after, she'd be giving him the best food. Making him all kinds of shit he liked. Why didn't Mac do that for me?"

His mind had an answer for that too. *Because she's not your mom. And when you hit her like you did, you kept her from making a living. Besides, she never cooked your favorite foods. Ever.*

That was right. She could put together a fine salad, but he was a man and men liked meat. Walton never really cared for beef. He thought it was because he'd grown up on a beef

143

ranch. His daddy had been the foreman there, and they had red meat with every meal, including breakfast. Walton swore that as soon as he left home, he was never eating it again.

But she cooked it for you, didn't she? Cooking something you must have told her a hundred times you didn't like. His mind was making him angrier and he told it to hush. *No, you need to be ready for anything when you get there. She's not going to be all lovely dovey just because you're hurting. You hurt her enough and she'll come around.*

"I don't know about that. When I knocked her around before, she got all violent with me too. Do you remember that?" He told himself that he did. "I had to have fourteen stitches in my arm when she hit me with that wine glass. What the fuck was she thinking?"

Women. Yes, that about summed it up for him. They were nuts. And it didn't matter about the subject either. They just were.

It was dinner time when he found the house. Blood was dripping down his leg. His cock wasn't just painful now, but he could no longer feel his hips. Holding onto the tree, he breathed into his mouth and out of his nose for a few minutes, then did the opposite when that didn't work. By that time, he was dizzy with not breathing right, and his belly was sick again. Moving slowly, he saw the man on the porch before he did the woman getting out of the car.

"Hello, Walton. Did you know that you're bleeding?" He looked at his ex-wife and wondered what the hell she'd done. It had to be all that rich living to make her look like she was shining. "What do you want? I've told your cohorts that I'm not going to let them hurt me again. And you can take that to the bank."

"You did this to me." Mac asked him how he had come to that conclusion. "You cursed me or something. You have to fix my pecker. It's going to come off if I don't get some relief soon. It.... I'm fucking not kidding you, Mac. Fix my dick."

He pulled out his gun and pointed it right at her. Then when she just stood there, he pointed at the man on the porch. Walton wasn't sure that he could hit him, but he could surely scare the shit out of him and make her do her duty toward him.

"What did you do to yourself? Jerk off one too many times?" He didn't hear a drop of concern in her voice for him, and he told her to come to him. "No. You're not going to order me around again, jackass. I don't have to listen to you."

"What if I kill that new husband of yours? I'd bet you'd be Johnny on the spot then, wouldn't you?" Mac just stood there. "I'm telling you, Mac, I fucking hurt and I want something for it. You have to fix me. I ain't peed in two fucking days."

"Let me see it." She wanted him to expose himself? In front of her husband? "Either you show me what you've done or you're shit out of luck."

"Mac, I swear to Christ, I hate you right now. I ain't fucking showing that man my dick. Get over here and fix me." She asked him if he knew what would happen if he didn't pee soon. "No, I don't fucking know. And I don't care. You did this, now fix me or so help me, I'll fucking kill you both."

"Yes, you go on ahead and do that, you moron. Let's see who fixes you then. You are the dumbest mother fucker I have ever encountered." He fired a shot at the man, but he didn't move. Nor did Mac. But she did laugh, and he fired the gun at her.

He wasn't sure who had moved first, Mac or who he

145

thought was her husband. But they came at him like he'd fired them from his gun, not a bullet. Walton felt himself falling backwards…his head hurt, but not nearly as badly as his dick did when the towel touched him. Then there was a fucking huge cat, a jaguar, sitting on his chest.

"What the fuck is this? The zoo let out? Please, I beg of you, kill me right now. If I'm gonna die, I want to do it because you tore my throat out and not because my dick explodes." The man from the porch moved up by his head. "Help me. I think this thing is gonna kill me."

"No. Not yet, at any rate. She did it well, don't you think? I didn't even know that she could shift into a cat yet. But she's beautiful, isn't she? I'm Dustin McCullough, by the way." Walton told him he didn't give a fuck who he was. "Well, you should. I'm the husband you just threatened to kill. And this cat is my wife."

Walton looked at the large teeth. He supposed there was more to the cat than that, but all he could see was how sharp and lethal looking they were. When the massive number of teeth moved closer to his head, he whimpered. Walton also felt his pecker let go of whatever it had been storing up. And it didn't release gently either.

He cried and screamed until the cat dug its sharp claws into his chest. Walton hurt. More than that, he was sick once more. Turning his head to puke, he cried again, telling himself when this was over, he was going to go on a big safari hunt and kill every cat within miles of him. And any kittens, they were dead —

"Walton, you're babbling." He snapped his mouth closed when Dustin laughed at him. "Now, as I was saying, Mackenzie said to tell you that you'll leave here and never return or she'll just let you die here."

"No. She has to fix me. I'm hurting." Dustin told him that she didn't care about that. That he'd hurt her a great deal too. "My dick is gonna fall off. A man cannot live without a dick. Tell her that."

"She can hear you." He didn't care. Walton wasn't sure if the stupid animal was Mac or not, but if she could fix him, he'd believe anything they wanted him to. "Tell her that I need her to fix me or so help me, I'll kill her."

The gun. He felt it in his hands just as he was begging for help. Moving slowly, he pulled it to his chest, and as carefully as he could, he pointed it at the cat's chest. Begging her once more, he cried when he told her that he was gonna kill her if she didn't help him. Dustin told him she wasn't going to do a damned thing.

"Fuck you then." Pulling the trigger, he felt satisfaction for the first time in a long time. The sound was incredibly loud, but when the cat leapt off him, he knew a sense of peace. Then the pain in his body just floated away.

In a very movie like quality, he saw his body lying there, his dick exposed and bloodied, his arms stretched out from his headless form. The big cat was there, staring at him with blood all over her fur, its face covered in it. But she wasn't hurt. There wasn't any blood on her chest where he knew that he'd shot her.

Getting weaker, he knew that he was dead. And on some level, he knew that he should be upset. But the agony in his dick was gone. His body no longer pained him. Walton closed his eyes and knew that he'd not hurt like that again. And that Mac had killed him.

Chapter 11

Dustin wasn't sure what to do. Mackenzie had been wandering around the house for several days now, not talking much and eating less. He looked at his mom when she said his name. Hugging her, just wrapping himself around his mom, made him feel a good deal better than he had before.

"Is she doing any better?" He shook his head. "I've come to talk to her, and I'll get rough with her. I want you to go with your dad. He's out in the truck. He and Colin are going vehicle shopping, and you need to get your wife one too."

"I don't want to leave her." She pulled away from him, and he could see the other two women in his family. "Don't hurt her. She's grieving in a way that I can't reach."

"No, she's not grieving, Dustin. She killed someone." Frowning at Lauren, he told her that he didn't understand the statement. Death was death. "It's her duty to heal, not kill. Like mine was to kill, not heal. She's not grieving for his death, but that she did it."

"Will she come out on the other side of this?" Reese smiled

149

at him. "Don't hurt her, please? Whatever is going on, she's in pain and it's killing me."

"We'll take care of her." He wasn't sure that he should leave her in the hands of these women. He loved them to pieces, but he was terrified of them. He looked at his mom as she continued speaking to him. "Go…go with your brothers and your dad. I won't let these girls hurt her. Only in that they'll talk and she'll listen."

He went to the truck and was surprised to see that his other brothers were there as well. Getting in the one his dad was in, he didn't feel any better about going than he had a few minutes ago. Before he could get out and return to his home, Colin started the truck and left the drive. They were on the road when he turned to his dad.

"She's hurting so badly. It's like a blanket around her." Dad said that he understood that. "I don't. She needs me, and I don't know what to do for her. And I'm worried that she's not eating well. It's like she doesn't care."

"You're helping her by doing this right now." He nodded at his dad. "Right before your mom and I were to be married, she was feeling a little down. Her mom had passed the week before, and I think she didn't want to go through with the wedding, it being a celebration and all. But my mom—not a nice person, by the way—she bullied her into doing it. I think she told her something along the lines of not to do it. Your mom was so mad about the conversation that I think she married me for spite. Don't care how it happened, but I'm sure glad it did."

"That does sound like Grandma." Colin laughed as he continued. "I think she did the same thing to me about playing football. Told me it was a girly sport and that I'd be better off being a cheerleader than playing such a stupid game. I played my heart out that year, and she patted me on the cheek when I made the state team. Like she'd been responsible for it."

"She was. And if you had asked her about it, she'd go on about how it was all her idea too. Damned woman." Dad rarely cursed, and to hear him now made Dustin laugh. "There's my boy. Yes, she was a tyrant, but she was smart about stuff. Like her slick way of making others do what they didn't want to."

"She gave me the ring that I asked Mackenzie to marry me with." Dad said that he had seen that. "I don't know what to do with Mac, Dad. I love her, and her being in this sort of pain is beyond what I know how to fix. And I need to."

"Sometimes — and this is from your mom — sometimes you can't fix it the right way. You have to go about it from behind and fix it. I wasn't sure what she meant, but then, I rarely do anymore. Durn woman is driving me batty with all her —" Colin cleared his throat. "Oh yeah. Anyway, she said that you have to get the person to realize that what they did wasn't wrong by telling them how badly they messed up. I'm thinking she might be right, but I won't tell her that. She's got a big enough head as it is. Love her to pieces, but she sure can be hard on a man sometimes."

He wasn't sure that she'd done a thing wrong. Defending herself shouldn't make her feel bad. But he supposed, too, that he could see Lauren's point. Mackenzie was a doctor first and foremost.

Dustin got out of the truck when they stopped. He watched his dad make a beeline right to the bigger trucks and had to laugh. For a man who didn't want a new one, he sure had his eye on the biggest in the lot. And it was bright red too.

151

"Dad is gonna crap a brick when he figures out that I already bought him that." He looked over at Colin and asked him if he was serious. "Yes. Lauren picked it out yesterday. She said that it was perfect for Dad, and that she could see him driving the kids around in it since it has the extended cab"

"What will Mom say?" He pointed to the large SUV next to it, equally large and just as red. "You'll have to let me know how hard she hits you then hugs you for it. I'm thinking that you're going to be a hero and a bad boy all at once."

"I can take it. By the way, we all bought it. If you want to, that is?" He said that he'd love to help out. "Good. I already put your name on the cards. When you have children, you'll want them to be safe too. I'm terrified every time Dad goes out with one of them. Their car isn't much better than the company truck."

He had to agree with him on that. Just yesterday he'd had to replace the floorboard with another piece of cardboard for his dad so he'd not lose the nails he'd picked up for them at the hardware store. Then last week he'd helped his mom set the emergency brake so her car wouldn't roll down the little hill at the high school she was working at.

They could afford better, and could certainly have something that wasn't constantly falling apart, but he, like his parents, used things until they were nearly ready to be dust before spending money on new. At least it was like that until he'd met Mackenzie. Now he wanted her to have the best of everything. He caught himself looking at the SUVs on the lot.

"That one will get her around in the winter." He asked Boyd how much traveling they did in the winter months. "Don't know yet, but I can see us needing something like

152

that to get around in. I got me one just last weekend. I had it outfitted with some extras too. Like I have a refrigerated container in the back for meds should I need them, as well as a kit that hangs on the back of the seat so I can have whatever I need even if I don't have my own bag."

"Can they do that here? I mean, should she need it?" He said that she would and that they did. "Okay, I'll do that then. What color is yours? You know what? Never mind. I might as well get me something too. In the event that I have to travel with the kids."

"You will need something better than what you have, yes." He nodded and waited for his brother to continue. "She's going to be all right."

"I hope so. I've never dealt with this before. Have you?" When he didn't answer, Dustin looked at his brother. "Have you, Boyd?"

"Yes, my first patient. It was when I was still in med school, and I might have quit then but for Mom. She got me on the right path and I did better after that." Dustin said she was bothered by killing that man. "Yes, so was I. I hadn't meant to. And had I been out of my first year, I might have been kicked out of school. But my teacher left me alone on a shift, and a bad accident brought in too many for me not to be put to work. I overdosed a patient. It might have happened to anyone. I hadn't any idea that he was already on drugs and wasn't told, or it might not have happened. But it did, and he died. You and Mom are the only ones that know. Unless she told Dad, which I wouldn't doubt."

Neither would Dustin. Mates, he'd come to realize early in life, told each other everything. And not only that, they were truthful about it as well. No sugar coating when they spoke, just plain hard facts.

Dustin ordered Mackenzie the all-terrain vehicle, and let Boyd tell them what he wanted done to the back of it. He had extra shocks put on it, as well as a tow hitch. Boyd was going to have the same thing done to his. By the time he was ready to leave, he had purchased two vehicles, and had asked for them to let him know when a camper came in. He thought that he and Mackenzie could enjoy a little getaway if they had one to just go with.

Twice he'd felt Mackenzie's anger, and both times he asked her if she was all right. She said she was fine, but didn't elaborate. He didn't ask either when she told him she was going to kill his family. He thought that was better left to them to deal with, as he was afraid that she might follow through on her threat when this was done. He, his brothers, and dad went to dinner. Dustin thought it was going to be a long night.

~~~

Mackenzie didn't talk to them when they all arrived en masse. She did watch them as they talked amongst themselves. Her heart wasn't into being social today. She'd murdered a man, and that was something that she never thought she'd have to deal with.

Having them die while she was taking care of them was normal, she thought. And having someone die on the operating table was something that she'd dealt with several times in her career. But she'd made her hand into a weapon, a long sharp blade, and had sliced it across Walton's throat, like he was nothing more than a pesky fly that she had to deal with.

When she'd been a large cat, Mackenzie had enjoyed

the power that it had given her. She also knew that she was dangerous, as well as heavier than her human self. Dustin told her she was beautiful, had commented on how she'd gone from person to cat very easily. But then Walton had shot her and she'd fought back.

You going to let every little thing bother you? You have never struck me as a whiny person. Nor a pussy. She knew whose voice was in her head. Hawk had been talking to her for several hours now. Mostly she'd been able to ignore him, but with the others there, she was having a hard time concentrating on one thing. *You do know that had you not killed him when you did, that he would have hurt Dustin and anyone else that was nearby when he was released? Also, and I'm sure you're aware of this, you killed him because he'd left you no choice in the matter. It was kill him or someone else would have been killed, another human or a child. Simple as that.*

Go away. His laughter did not have a bit of humor in it. *I don't like you, remember? You and I are enemies. Go about your business and leave me to mine.*

No. We're a lot alike if you ask me. Stubborn as hell. Meaner than a rattlesnake when cornered or not. I think I'm just mean, but then my momma loves me. Mackenzie didn't know how he'd come up with that, so said nothing. *Also, and you're going to find this very hard to believe, but you impressed me.*

How so? She shifted on her seat and all the women turned and looked at her. *I feel as if I'm on trial or something. But instead of being found guilty of a crime, your family, the women in it, are trying their best to make me see that I did nothing wrong. I want them to go the fuck away and leave me to my grief. Not grief, but something.*

You didn't do anything wrong. She snorted at him. *I have a*

155

story or two to tell you. One that you're not going to care for, but I'm telling you anyway. It's about the other women in my family. Lauren for example. Did you know that she lived in a house that had no running water or any heat? And that she lived with her parents, who would beat her and each other to the point of near death? And that she had a single coat and a pair of shoes that she had to turn in each day after coming home, and wouldn't get them until the next school day? When she left home, she was barefoot and coatless because she was terrified to ask for them. Before that she had saved up pop cans, and filled them with sand and dirt that she found after digging out a hole to hide in. The Burchers took her in when she made her way to their home one cold winter night.

Where are her parents now? Hawk said they were dead, thankfully. *Did she do it? I don't know why I think this, but she'd never hurt them. Someone else killed them for her. I know that she's killed before — I'd have to be a fool not to know that — but she didn't kill her flesh and blood. She's not like that. So, who did it for her?*

No, she'd not do that, you're right in that. Victoria. The reason that they're friends, good friends. Victoria was being hurt by them. Tied to a barn wall and left there to meet the sun. Lauren helped her escape, and in return — or perhaps she didn't know this at the time — Victoria killed them. The Burchers, her adoptive parents, have never treated her as anything but their blood child. She said nothing, but felt her anger get the better of her. *You're scaring Dustin. He thinks that my mom and the others are pissing you off.*

After telling Dustin she was fine, Mackenzie asked about Reese. *I know that she's had a hard time of it, and that she used to be a trucker.*

Yes, she helped Jon escape from the lab that he was in. They did things to him, most of which we'll never know about, and made him what he is today. Mackenzie told him that she was like him in some ways. That the blood that they shared had changed her in ways she wasn't sure of yet. *I know. So am I. It's what I'm doing today, trying to figure out what happened to me when you and he saved my life.*

I didn't do anything that anyone else wouldn't have done for you. He laughed and she felt her face heat up. *What about Reese? You said she had a time of it.*

Yes, she did. For a few years she kept Jon safe all on her own, working odd jobs until the men from the lab found them. Driving sometimes as many as forty hours straight just to keep ahead of them. And in all that time, it never occurred to her that she could just quit. It was in her heart to save him. No matter the cost. Mackenzie looked at the other women in the family. *You might want to know a bit about my mom too, but that's her story to tell. I will let you in on something that she doesn't know I know. My mom is terrified of guns. She can use one, thanks to Lauren, but she is terrified that she's going to fire on the wrong person and kill them.*

I would be as well. He told her that her cat and the things that were now a part of her body were no different. *I can't put a safety on my body, Hawk. I'm dangerous.*

No, not dangerous, but aware. She asked him what he meant. *A dangerous person is one that doesn't care if they harm anyone when they're upset. An aware person keeps those he loves safe, beyond anything that might happen to them. You did that the other day. And I for one think you should get over yourself and talk to the others. You're scaring them. My mom thinks you'll leave her all alone. Not that she doesn't have the rest of us, but she's taken a shine to you.*

Your mom is a sweetheart with the heart of a lion. Or a bear. Hawk agreed with her. *I don't know what to do, Hawk. I want to be glad that I killed him, but I killed him.*

You did. And you should know that had you not killed him, he would have tried to kill you and Dustin. I'm not just saying that, but Jon told me. It was in his head to end your life, and that of your mate, simply because he could. She stared at the wall, not really seeing it when Hawk continued. *I just figured out that I can hear the thoughts of a fucking tree.*

Laughter burbled from her mouth. The others stared at her and smiled. She felt better now. Mackenzie had no idea why, but she did. She told them that she was talking to Hawk about what she'd done.

"I'm sure that he had plenty of insight on this sort of thing. However, you should know that none of us feel that you've done anything wrong. Why, any one of us could have been hurt had you not done what you did. And when he shot at you...well, I nearly had a heart attack myself." Bea sat beside her after moving to the trolley that was filled with fruit and cupcakes. "You should eat something, dear. I know that Dustin is very worried for your health."

Mackenzie ate the offered cookies and cupcake, feeling like she'd not eaten in several days. She supposed that she hadn't. Depression had hit her hard. Just as she was ready to admit that she'd been silly in all this, Lauren started talking.

"You do know that no one cares that he's dead, don't you? I mean, I suppose you might a little. He was your husband for a little while. But now? I don't think so." Mackenzie agreed that there wasn't anyone to mourn his passing. "And you did what you had to do."

"Yes, I understand that now. I don't like the fact that I killed him, but I do know he left me no choice. But, that doesn't mean that I can't be upset over it." Lauren nodded. "Walton wasn't a nice person, and he'd not been in my heart for a long time. But as you said, we were married, and in... something. I'm not sure now that it was love, but we were happy for a little while."

"What happened? I mean, if you don't mind sharing with us. I, for one, would like to know what turned him into a turd." They all laughed at Bea, who grinned with them. "I don't usually curse. I find it to be sort of scary for me. And something I'm not terribly good at. But you girls, you sure have a handle on it."

"You are right about that." Lauren kissed Bea on the cheek, then ate two cookies. "But share away. I knew him. Not well, but I knew the kind of man he was."

"No, he wasn't a good soldier, nor was he a good person. Especially after he got a taste for drugs. Nothing bad at first, but when he was hurt they prescribed him some hefty pain killers. I wouldn't have, but then I wasn't in charge of his care." She told them what he was taking. "Anyway, after that, he thought that I could make sure that he had enough drugs to sell. And that was when he started knocking me around. He had it in his head to be a drug lord in the service. It, like a lot of his plans, never panned out."

"When he put you in the hospital, why wasn't he discharged the first time?" Mackenzie should have known that Lauren would have found out everything about her time in the service. "I'm sorry. I know that he hit you several times before you reported it."

"Yes, I was a fool. The first time...well, as some women do, I felt that it was my fault. Of course I know better now, but the second time he did it he was high, and while that isn't an excuse, I did give him one more chance. The third time was the final straw. He beat me badly enough that I was put in the hospital for several days. When he was arrested and put in irons, I filed for and got my divorce. That didn't stop him from beating me to shit, but it did get him away from me when the military found out about it." She thought of something and turned to Reese. "You said that someone was looking into the insurance policy that he had. What ever happened about that?"

"We don't know who he hired, and he more than likely killed the person that collected on it. An elderly woman is all we know for sure. The policy, of course, has been nullified, but since he had nothing and is dead, it doesn't look like anyone is going to be able to collect it back." Mackenzie asked if they'd come after her for it. "No, they can't. You two were divorced before the policy was taken out, and they're sort of at fault on their own for not checking to see if she was living."

"That's sad. I'm assuming that everyone is thinking that the woman is dead, like you said. Hopefully she didn't have family that is looking for her or wondering where she is." Reese nodded and said that it was very sad. "And what about the other man? The one that he used to fake his death?"

"He was a homeless man. I can't remember his name right now, but he was hired to take the car to that point and wait for his return ride back to town. It, of course, never came, and his body was determined to have been Walton's simply because it was in the car registered to him. As for the paperwork that was misfiled as well as incomplete, that's been taken care of as well. We know that a woman Walton was seeing let him in one night to have sex on her desk. The recordings of it show Walton taking her key after he drugged her, and then changing out the needed documents. He was pretty slick about it. The woman has been fired and charged with all kinds of shit that she deserved." Mackenzie thought of all the lives that Walton had fucked up in his quest for money. "Men and women both have done more for less. You should know that too."

"I do, but it makes it no less depressing, don't you think?" She sat and talked to them for another hour. It was getting dark now, and she just wanted to go to sleep. It had been a long few days and her body was aching with exhaustion. At some point, she supposed, she had fallen asleep, because the next thing she knew, Dustin was carrying her up to bed.

Chapter 12

Boyd kept an eye on Mackenzie when she was around, but didn't interfere with her working. She was doing fine, and he was enjoying bouncing ideas or issues that he found off her. If he was honest with himself, he was sort of in awe of her. She knew more and had done more in her career than he'd ever do in his whole life.

"Dr. Boyd?" He looked up at Myrtle, his nurse, and wondered why she seemed so concerned. "There's a woman in one of the rooms. She's in labor. But.... I have called an ambulance and the police, but I don't think she's gonna make it."

He told her to get Mackenzie as he made his way to the little room that served as a prenatal room. As soon as he stepped into the room, he knew that Myrtle was right. The woman wasn't going to survive whatever had happened to her.

"I'm hurting." He told her that he could see that, and made his way to her side. "The baby is coming, and I know

163

that I'm gonna die. I've been hurt bad. You have to save him. He's all I got left in this world. Please?"

"Who did this?" He was surprised that she was still conscious. Or able to talk around the wounds on her face for that matter. "Miss? What is your name?"

"Don't matter. I ran as far as I could, but he found me. I killed him this time. But he hurt me bad. Please? You gotta save my baby." He asked her again for her name and she simply fainted.

"Christ." He nodded at Mackenzie as he started prep work to deliver the child. "Who did this?"

"She told me that she managed to kill him this time, but won't tell me her name." They worked together, Mackenzie setting up the operating area, him taking care of the woman. Once he got her undressed, he could see that she had fought hard at her battle to save her baby.

There were several stab wounds on her chest. Bruising on her belly too. A perfect outline of a boot. By the time the police arrived with their camera, they had washed up some of the wounds and were stitching them closed. Boyd didn't think it was going to do any good in saving her, and if she didn't survive, he wanted to say that he'd done his very best for her.

"You think she'll make it?" He told the officer that he was going to try. "We found a body about an hour ago. Could be who she killed. He's beaten to shit too, but not like this. A stab to his heart. He wouldn't have gone down easily."

When her heart stopped, they cut her open. There was little time now…it was the baby they were working to save. Not that they wouldn't keep trying, but the child wouldn't survive where he currently was. As soon as the little boy was delivered, Boyd took care of him…there was some bruising on his little body too. Mackenzie tried to save the woman. She found a small nick to her aortic artery, but the woman was long gone before they could do anything to save her life.

The police took pictures and made notes on the condition of not only the woman, but the child too. He was fine, other than beaten up a little from when his mom was. Boyd made notes on those injuries as well for the record. It was the quickest, as well as the hardest, hour of his life.

"We don't have a place for him to go when he's released." Boyd had already figured that out. The child services that were in place in their town could only care for toddlers and up. This child would need constant care for a while. "You think your mom and dad will help us out a bit again?"

"I can ask them. I'm sure that they will." Boyd reached for his mom and told her what was going on. "She said she'd be glad to help him out. Mom said that she and Dad would take care of everything with him."

"Good people, your parents." Joe Windfall, the officer in charge, looked down at the little guy. "Who would do this to a little baby, Boyd? I mean, it's bad enough that he killed the mom, but to have hurt this little guy, no matter how indirectly, is a shame."

"I agree. Do you have a name on the man?" He said that he had his wallet and they were looking for next of kin. "She outlived him, so if there is any insurance, someone will have to set it up for the boy here. Poor woman. I haven't any idea how she made it this far. Even coming from out on the sidewalk should have killed her right away, but she had someone powerful watching over her today. I'm thinking that it was a little bit of motherly love, too. She told us to save him first, but she didn't tell me her name."

"There something else we should do right now? DNA. I think, should there be any family on his side or hers, they'll want proof that she is who she is and that the child is hers and the man's." Joe thought that was a great idea and told Mackenzie that. "I can do both right now, since you're here. The man...I'm assuming that they'll need to do an autopsy on him, and we can do it then as well. It's not for proof so much as getting to the bottom of things, right?"

"I like that. Covering all our asses is a good thing." Boyd led his mom and dad into his office and brought the baby to them when they arrived. Joe followed and spoke to them. "I sure do appreciate you doing this for us again, Mr. and Mrs. McCullough. You know that the city will reimburse you for whatever you need. This little man will need some care, no doubt about that."

"You don't have to do that. Whatever we need, we're glad to give. Do you have a name for him?" Boyd said that they didn't, but would have to call him John Doe for now. "What a sad name. Hopefully he has himself some family out there that can come and give him a good solid one. To be such a little thing and not to have a soul to love you...We'll take care of that right now. Won't we, Rich? Show him right from the start what his momma did for him by coming to our family."

As they cuddled with the little man, he went back to the room where the woman lay. Mackenzie was cleaning her up, making sure that she was ready to leave them. When she started to put the things that the woman had been wearing into a bag to go to the police station, a small wallet slipped out and onto the floor.

Neither of them touched it, but called for Joe to come back.

When he picked it up after taking a few pictures of it and where it had come from, he was careful about fingerprints by wearing gloves. Joe looked inside and told them each thing he found, and Boyd wrote it down. There was four dollars, as well as a note. Boyd asked him if he was going to read it to them.

"I shouldn't. But I'm gonna. It says 'To whoever finds me dead. Call my brother here to fetch me. He'll not take my little Samuel, but he will make sure that he has a nice pot to piss in.' Then there is a number on how to reach out to him, and her name. Norine Jacobson."

"The man's body, is it Jacobson?" Joe nodded, but looked grim. Boyd glanced around the room, at the body still there as well as the pitiful clothing she'd had on, and then spoke again. "What is it, Joe? Something we should know about?"

"Probably not, but I'm gonna tell you on account'a it's too hard for me to hold it together. Her brother, Peter Amos, died about a week ago. Car accident. The only reason I know about it, because he's not from around here, is because it happened right outside our jurisdiction. It was an accident, not his fault. Texting and driving by the other driver took him out." Boyd asked if there was a wife or any other family. "No, not that I know of. I'll be looking, but I'm thinking that I heard that he'd only had the one sister. We're looking into Jacobson's family, but not having a lot of luck. There is one name associated with him, Basil Jacobson, but we can't find hide nor hair of him."

"If it won't offend you, I'll have Lauren look. She has some pretty extensive contacts." Joe said he'd appreciate that. "Also, this little boy...we have a name for him. Do you mind if we go ahead and file his birth certificate? It'll make it easier now that we know at least that much. We can fill in the name of the father later, after the tests come back."

"That'll be fine with me. Samuel Jacobson it is then." Joe looked at the woman as they stood there. Since Mackenzie had cleaned her up, instead of looking better, her wounds just looked starker, more violent. "What do you suppose could possess a man to hurt someone they are married to like this? And her carrying his son? I mean, just look at her. She looks like she's been beaten for a long time, doesn't she?"

"I would say that she's been beaten a great deal over the last several years. Especially over the last year of her life. There are scars on most of her body that are still new. There are even a few in her hairline, as well as her legs and back." Mackenzie showed them the one that was on her hip. "This alone should have put her in the hospital for a long time. I'm betting at least a month. It looks like a gunshot wound to me. If not, then it's something close."

When the van showed up to take her body to the hospital, his parents were questioned as well by the county. Could they care for the little boy? Did they know that he was going to be up at night? And they were told who to call should there be any problems. Samuel was taken to the emergency room as well to be checked over, they told them. Boyd left to go to the hospital to perform the task of doing the autopsy on the woman. Mackenzie went with him, saying she'd help.

Three hours later, they were finished. The findings were horrific, far worse than they had thought. Not only had she been shot, but her leg had been broken before and not properly set. Her jaw had been wired shut for a time, but again, hadn't healed correctly. Mackenzie had surmised that it had been taken out by someone other than a doctor. The woman had endured a great deal before her death, and Boyd hoped that someone would find justice for her.

Boyd was called to the nurse's station just as he was leaving the hospital.

"There's a phone call for you. Not you directly, but for the coroner. You want to take it?" He nodded at the nurse there, too tired to explain to her that he was only the acting coroner until they found someone to take the job. "Go ahead, Dr. Boyd. Line three when you're ready. And so you know, we've taken up a little collection for the little boy. No way to start life out with nobody to love you proper-like."

He said his name in the phone, and the person on the other end started barking orders at him. "I swear to Christ, if I get transferred again, I'm going to have someone for my dinner. I don't have time for this shit, and I'm in no mood for any scam that Axel has going. He's my cousin, not my fucking kid. Though there are times when he acts just like one."

When she paused to take a breath, or so he thought, Boyd cut her off. "My name is Dr. Boyd McCullough. And since I don't have the slightest clue what you're talking about, I'm going to wait before telling you if this is a scam or not." She sighed heavily, and he could almost feel her exhaustion and anger. "Can we start over?"

"Someone called here looking for me. A...let me look. Joe Windfall. He said that he needed to talk to me. Calling his office got me transferred...well, this is the fourth person that I've talked with to try to figure out what the fuck is going on." He asked her name. "Virginia. Well, it's Virginia Basil Jacobson, but the only person that ever called me Basil was Axel. My cousin. Whatever he's done, I have nothing to do with him. I got enough shit going on right now that I don't need whatever snake oil he's trying to sell on my docket."

169

"I'm sorry that I have to tell you this, Miss Jacobson, but he is dead." The silence at the other end had him hurrying to fill in the quiet. "His wife too. She died giving birth to her son, Samuel. He's going to be fine, but he's going to need someone to care for him."

"Did he kill her? Norine, did he kill her?" He said that he wasn't able to say. "I understand. I talked to her once. I didn't know she was going to have a baby, but I told her to get away from him. Axel is bad news to everyone he meets. And it doesn't matter if he's related to them or not."

"I'm sorry." He heard the shuffle of papers, then a door close. "I don't know where you are, Miss Jacobson, but I'm glad that someone found you. We knew there was a relative around, but not who."

"I tried my best to keep out of his life. It is...it was a nightmare and a catastrophe from the get go. Norine was a nice person. She and Axel were unsuited, but to know that there is a child makes me think that she might not have been able to get away far enough. Can you tell me what happens to him?" Boyd told her that he didn't know. They were hoping someone would come forward. "I know that she had a brother. His name was Peter Amos. Him I didn't know."

"I'm afraid that he's dead as well. Unrelated to these two." She didn't speak, but he waited this time. He wondered, other than the blood connection, what sort of other shit he'd done to this woman to make her dislike him so much. Axel had beaten his wife, and as they had no proof of it, they could only assume that he'd done it before as well. It was a messy situation, regardless.

"I can come there if I need to, Dr. McCullough, but I'm in no position to take the baby. I'm sorry about that. If you need me to help out with money, I can do that. But I can't take the boy. I don't...I know nothing about children, and I wouldn't even have the slightest clue what he might need in the way of support." Boyd told her that someone would need to come here, eventually, but as far as the child was concerned, he didn't know as yet. "All right. I can be there in a few days. I can't stay long, but I can come out and make arrangements for them both. And pay whatever needs to be put together for the little boy. But that's all I can do. Nothing more. If you think you can talk me into something else, tell me now and I'll just send the money."

"No, I won't try to tell you to take him. If you don't want him, then that'll be fine too. I'm sure that there is someone out there that would like a newborn little boy." She told him he wasn't playing fair. "I'm not trying to do anything but answer your questions, Miss Jacobson. When you get your arrangements made, call me and I'll meet you at the airport."

After giving her his number, he told Mackenzie what was going on. She told him that Lauren just called and gave her information on the cousin. As well as what she did for a living.

"She writes. Blogs and books. I'm not sure what she makes off either, but she must be doing well for herself." Boyd told her what she was going to do. "I can understand not wanting a newborn. They're a great deal of work."

They both went back to work; the body of Axel Jacobson had arrived now and they were to do the same for his body. Cause of death was easy, Boyd thought. A stab to his heart was what killed him. Quick and clean. Not at all like what his wife had suffered.

~~~

Dustin came awake suddenly. His entire body was feeling

171

the climax that rattled his head. Holding onto Mackenzie, he cried out a second time when she swallowed him past the tightness of her throat.

"Christ, woman." She looked up at him, his cock deep in her mouth. "What are you doing, trying to kill me?" The small popping sound made him moan when she released him from her mouth.

"I thought you looked tense." He tried to pull her up to his body but she moved back. "I'm not finished yet. I need to feel you fucking my mouth. Then you can fuck me."

"I want to fuck you now." She laughed and he laid back, but steadied himself on his elbows to watch her. "I love the way you woke me. Sometime I'm going to do the same for you."

Dustin was having a hard time concentrating on his words. She was doing such delightful things to him and he didn't want her to stop. But when she sat up, her nakedness there for him to admire, he told her to come to him.

"I want to ride you." He helped her slide over him. He rocked upward when she was seated, and nearly cried out when she leaned over him and bit his nipple. "You taste amazing. I especially love the way your hot cum tastes when it slides down my throat."

"You're killing me." She giggled and he had to smile. "Anytime you want to come in here and wake me this way, it's fine by me."

"I had a rough day." He held her, not sure he could hold a conversation where he was going to be required to speak, when she told him she was coming. Watching her release was the best thing he'd ever seen.

Rolling her to her back, his cock still planted deep within

her, he suckled at her nipples, nipping at the tender flesh that was there for him. When Mackenzie wrapped her legs around his, he fucked her harder, not caring at all if he ever left this room again.

"Come for me, love. Let me watch you come to peak while I take you." She held him to her throat and he bit down. Not hard enough to draw blood, but she did cry out with a short climax.

As he licked along her jaw and throat, she held him tightly, both inside her body and out. Dustin watched her face while he pounded her harder, enjoying the way her breasts moved, and her mouth tightened when she was close. And when she bowed up from the bed, her eyes tightly closed and her mouth open in a scream, he bit her again, marking her not just with his teeth but his nails as well as he raked them down her back and hip.

Mackenzie came three more times, each time lovelier than the last. When she finally begged him to stop, to let her rest, he told her no, that it was his turn. He loved her, he realized, more than he ever had anyone or anything in his life. And when he came, his body melding with hers, he knew a kind of peace that he would enjoy forever.

They laid there for another hour, neither speaking, but touching and holding each other. Whatever had happened, he was sure that she'd tell him about it. If not, then he was all right with that as well. She was here now, and that's what was important to him.

"Your parents are watching an orphan for the next few days." He kissed her rather than asking. "His mom was beaten to death by her husband, and it nearly killed him as well. The man is dead. The only good that has come out of this whole thing."

"I'm sorry." Mackenzie nodded and said nothing else. "My parents have been doing that for a few years. I didn't know that they were still doing it, but I'm glad that they could help out. They loved watching the children."

"They had a set of rules, being that his parents are both dead. I don't know." He kissed her throat and held her. "We never talked that much about children. Do you want any?"

"I do. When you're ready. I don't have to go through what you do, so it's up to you to tell me when you want them. I would, however, like to be married first. I know that it's assumed that we are already, but I'd like to have it nice and legal." Mackenzie didn't say anything, so he changed the subject. "We have a buyer for the house we finished up today. Nearly double what we paid for it, but with the cost of us working on it, we're still going to do well with it. I'm having the crew come out tomorrow and finish up what we need done here. Then they're going to go to—"

"I'd like to have a child or two with you, but I would also like to adopt. I know that we'd have to be inspected and our lives looked into, but there are so many children out there like young Samuel, who need someone to love them." He didn't know who Samuel was for sure, but assumed it was the young boy his parents had. "What do you think of that idea?"

"Wonderful. I know that you're aware that Colin and Lauren have adopted their children. I don't know if I'd want to go with four at once, but I can see us taking in a few and raising them as our own." She nodded; he could feel her head moving under his chin as he held her. "Anything else going on that I need to know about?"

"I'm sure there is, but I'm too tired to think right now." He held her until she was asleep. It took her all of four minutes, he'd bet. When he moved to his back, taking her with him, Dustin reached for his mom to ask her how it was going.

Just wonderful. Samuel is coming home with us in an hour or so. He's got some bruises on him, but nothing life threatening. Your dad and I are going to keep him for a few days, then we'll see what happens. I guess he has no one left. Dustin told his mom what he and Mackenzie had talked about. *Do you think you'll take on this little guy? Well, it would be nice to keep him in the family. Your dad and I try so hard not to fall in love with these little guys, but we always do. Then it breaks our hearts for a time to let them go. But it's for the best…for all the children we care for.*

Because you're a great person, and so is Dad. She thanked him. *Mackenzie is doing better every day. I think whatever happened with you girls the other day, it was perfect.*

I'd like to take full credit for it, but I think it was mostly Lauren and Reese. Then there was Hawk. I'm pretty sure that you have him to thank for all of it. We did talk, but he had opened the door for us. And the girls, they talked and Mackenzie listened. Do you think she's going to be all right, son? He said that he thought so. *Good. She's such a sweet young woman. You couldn't have done better had I picked her out for you. Dad said that you are going to have the house sold in the morning. That's good for you.*

Yes. I think they've been watching us put the house together, so they knew just when we were ready. Not having to put it on the market is nice too. No open houses and people running in and out all the time. She congratulated him again. *We're ready for a new house project once we have done the work that you and Dad want, as well as the things here that need to be complete. Hawk's home is done too. Just needed a little sprucing up, and the furniture that he took gave it a nice homey look. When I saw him yesterday, he said that the flowers from you were a nice touch as well.*

I put some things in his pantry and icebox as well. I know that he's at our house a great deal, but he said he needed some alone time as well. But our house? I'll be glad to have this house done over. Just the dining room is needing to be enlarged. I'm thinking that with some of you being married now, it won't be long for the rest of them too. He thought of his brothers having mates, and knew it was a great idea too. But he was a little afraid for Hawkins' mate to come. She sounded, from Jon, like a real hellcat. He could not wait. *Why don't you and Mackenzie come over for dinner tonight? We can invite the rest of the family and have a nice cookout on the deck. It won't be long before it's going to be too cold for us to eat out there.*

I'll talk to Mackenzie when she wakes up. Mom told him he was smart for doing that. *Yeah, I don't want to get my hat handed to me when it's not necessary.*

After promising his mom that he'd ask Mackenzie first thing, he got up and went to the bathroom to clean up. It was going to be a short day today, getting things finalized at not just his parents' home, but at the new one and his too. As soon as he was dressed, he headed to the kitchen. Might as well get his day going, he told himself.

"The sooner we find a house to work on, the better it'll be." He smiled when he realized he was talking to himself. He supposed he'd picked that habit up from his dad.

Chapter 13

Larson looked at the different screens on his desk. He supposed that someone coming in and seeing his workstation would think him a wizard. But to him, it just made sense to have three screens going at once. That way he wouldn't miss a single thing while talking to clients. Mostly his family, but he did have a few others right now.

"I'd let it ride if I were you, Tom. There is a little downturn right now, but it'll pick up soon enough." Larson stretched his neck as he listened to Tom go on about profits and losses. "If you want to sell, I'd be happy to do that for you, but I'd keep it for a few more days."

"No. It's not that I don't trust you, Larson, but sell it all for me. I can't afford to take a hit like that if it doesn't return for me." He said that he'd do that and confirmed that he wanted it all sold at the price that was on his computer. Then Larson reminded him that their conversation was being recorded. "Yes, I'm aware of that. You have to cover your own ass in this. Yes, I'm confirming that I want to sell all my stock in

Ranger Mountains right now. Every share."

Larson did that, making a tidy profit for himself as well. When he was done, he told Tom that his money would be direct deposited as soon as he had the money. Tom told him that he trusted him. Then they moved on to less business talk and more friendly conversation.

"I got me a boat. Not the one that I wanted, but something similar. Donna and I are going to go out on it in a few days. I cannot wait." He asked him where they were going. "I don't know just yet. There is this firm that does that sort of thing with you. They come on the boat and run things for you, showing you how to navigate the seas and the boat too. A training vacation, if you will."

"That sounds good." Really? It sounded sort of stupid to him. Not the getting away part, but having a firm come onto your boat and run it for you? He wasn't that trusting. "You have everything in order then? I mean, names and numbers in case we need to reach you for anything?"

"Worrywart." Larson didn't try to deny it. "Yes, I've given everything to my business partner and my mom. Who is, by the way, watching the kids. Do you ever just cut loose?"

"No. Not ever. It's bad for business. I hope you have a wonderful time, Tom. Give my best to your wife." He said that he would and they'd have a great vacation. Especially thinking about him stuck in his office all the time. "You do that."

As he finished his work for the day, Larson stood up. Dinner with his family tonight, then tomorrow he was going to find someplace to live that wasn't a condo. Roots, he wanted roots, and a house was going to give that to him.

Picking up his notes on a few houses, he made his way to

his parents' home. But on the way, he spotted his dad in front of a house. Getting out, he stood beside him and stared at the mammoth home.

"I don't know. What do you think?" He asked his dad what he meant. "We're looking for another project. I, for one, feel this place is a mite too big for us. I mean, we can do it, but it'll not be a quick one. What do you think about it?"

"Can we see the inside of it?" His dad produced the keys and in they went. The huge wrap around porch was surrounded by a beautiful iron railing. The detail was amazing, and he loved that it was painted a dark color. "Dad, is that cast iron?"

"Yeah. It'll need to be sandblasted and repainted, not a lot of work, but some. There is this place we work with, they can take it down and fix it and put it back in a couple weeks. The wood is oak. Large planks like that would be hard to replace if you had to. But it looks all right." Larson nodded. "The door and the windows here on this floor are in good shape too. Know a guy that can replace the stained glass for little to nothing. It looks to me like it's only a couple of cracked pieces, not the whole design. I might even just leave it alone. Nothing wrong with it but that little bitty crack."

The entrance hall was better than he had imagined. The staircase came together at the base of a big decorative stained glass mural, then right as he walked in it divided in two and went to opposite sides of the house. The floor, more wood, was parquet, and looked like it had been redone recently. As they made their way around the bottom floor, he stood in the library and could see it filled with books. First editions, as well as mysteries, which he enjoyed.

"The kitchen will need a whole overhaul. And some

of the work in there will have to be done up to code. Got a nice farmer's sink in there that if somebody wanted it, they could make a few bucks off of. Also, it needs a couple more bathrooms. One on this floor, and I'd say at least two more on the second." He nodded at his dad as he continued. "There's a fireplace in the other room you could nearly roast a herd of cattle in. Mantle is nice, though. I think there is a lot to be said for a house like this one. But too big to make much in the way of profit on."

"Dad, I want this house." Dad stared at him with the oddest look on his face. "I've been looking for something much smaller, a couple of bedrooms, but this is what I want. This house."

"Son, you do know that something this size needs a family in it? At the very least a big staff. You'll be into some pretty nice sized money, too, when you have to take care of that yard. The back end of this place looks like it ain't been touched in decades." He nodded as they moved out of the library into a different part. "This room...now this is a dining room."

It was too. There was a corner cabinet at each corner. French doors that led out into a stone covered patio that was overgrown with weeds and a couple of trees. But he could see it. The view from this area alone would have him sitting in this room for hours on end. There was carpet down on the floor in here, and his dad bent at the waist and pulled up a corner of it. Hardwood floors, his dad said, that just needed some loving.

"How much?" Dad simply shook his head. "I mean, just for the house. The rest I can figure out as I go. I know I'll need it safe, but how much are they asking for it?"

"There is just a smidge over two hundred acres, Larson. What you thinking of doing with all that?" Larson told him he had no idea at this point. "It would come with the land and the house, plus, the barn that's back there, and you'll be getting a pond that is in the middle." He told him the price.

"Is that counting the work that you were talking about? I mean, the new furnace and air conditioner that you mentioned in the other room?" Dad said he'd give him a good deal on that. "I would hope you would, but I'm not concerned about that. Do you think it's worth the price?"

"No. I think they're a little on the high side, what with all the work that needs done. I mean, that's a slate roof up there, and it'll need to be replaced if you don't want.... Are you sure, son? This house?" He told him he'd never been so sure about anything in his life. "All right then. I'll go in and set you up with a good deal on it. The bank is wanting it off their books, so I don't think we'll do too bad on that. As soon as it's done, we'll go in and fix the necessaries now, and then work on the rest as we get to it."

They walked around the inside of the house again, this time climbing the beautiful staircase. When they reached the second level, his dad found the stairs to another level that had been blocked off. Up there they found a dance room. Dad was thrilled with the original wallpaper, as well as the oak flooring and windows.

"Thought this was just the attic space. And that furniture over there, you'll be able to use some of that too. Or you can sell it off. You want it?" He told him he wanted to stick with old things in the house if he could, to keep it right with the house. "Yeah, don't blame you there. Hawkins took a bunch of old stuff from that closed up antique store, but there's a bit more of it you can go through if you want it. Your mom, she wheedled them down to almost nothing."

By the time they were in the kitchen again, he had a list of things that needed to be done, along with a price it would cost to fix or repair it. In addition to the third floor, they found an entire room full of furniture, as well as some rolled up carpets. They didn't touch any of it—Larson didn't own it yet—but Dad said he'd make sure that everything in the house stayed with it. Larson was in the yard again when he noticed the six-car garage and the carriage house nearby that looked like it served as an apartment to it. He was walking around the overgrown gardens when his dad came to find him.

"You gotta go down to the bank in the morning and go over the paperwork. You just bought yourself a house. I'm right proud of you." He wanted to dance, something he was never any good at. Hugging his dad, he was so excited that he actually did a little jig. "You're gonna need to settle up on what you want done first. I'd start on the furnace and air, then the roof."

"Okay. You set up a time and I'll be here. I was thinking, since I don't do anything like you guys, I'd work on the yard. I can pull weeds with the best of them." Dad suggested that he find someone that knew weeds or flowers. "Good idea. I'll call the local nursery and see what they can do to help out. Dad, you have no idea how excited I am."

"I can see it on you." Larson looked around the yard, the expansiveness of it. "You sure got your work cut out for you. The house is solid and doesn't need much in structure, but it's a mess out here. You'll surely have a showplace when you're done with it. I'm glad that you're taking it on. It needs a man like you, one that has the vision to make it look like its glory days."

"Yes, I can almost see it. I know that it's going to be a great deal of work, as you said, but I own it, and that's what I really needed." Dad hugged him again. "Okay, now I have to find myself a mate. That way she can share in some of the work."

They were both laughing as they made their way to their cars. Larson was only kidding. A mate? Never. Not that he didn't want one, but he knew that he wasn't much of a catch. He was set in his ways, stubborn, and liked things in place. The house, he knew, was going to drive him insane with the work, but he also knew that he could handle a little mess when the bigger picture was right there for him to see. He was a homeowner.

~~~

Mackenzie looked at the envelope in front of her again. This was the third time that she'd tried to read it over and gotten distracted. Well, not distracted, but she didn't want to think about it. Nothing in the office was helping, just her mind drifting away again and again. When her door opened, she was almost glad for the physical distraction. Her mind wasn't anyplace she wanted to be at the moment.

"Are you busy?" She just frowned at Parker. He'd been absent of late; bringing in the crops was time consuming and took a lot out of a guy. "I have something I need to ask you. Not medical, but just a man to a woman sort of question."

"No, babies don't come from cabbage patches, nor do you go blind masturbating too much." He stared at her, then burst out laughing. "I had a fourteen-year-old in here earlier asking those questions of me. Who tells them this crap?"

"I think it might be written on the bathroom wall or

something. I believe teachers tell them that too, so they don't catch them at it. But I knew that about the babies. I grow cabbage, and have never seen a newborn under one of the plants. No, this isn't medical. I want to get Reese something special for Christmas." She reminded him it was a couple of months away. "Yeah, I know that too, but this will take some planning on my part. I want to take her on a long cruise."

"That would be lovely. Especially to get her away from the cold here. Where are you going to go?" He told her that was where she came in. "Oh. You're looking for ideas on where to go. I think I can help you with that. You should take her to Europe and travel down the rivers there and see the country."

"How long will we be gone?" She told him there were different plans for whatever he wanted to see. "I like that. Okay, that was very helpful. By the way, you and Dustin will have Thanksgiving this year, and Christmas will be at my parents'. It's tradition. Well, the Christmas is, but the Thanksgiving thing is new. It came about when we started having mates. If you need help, you can ask Reese. I'd avoid Lauren if I were you. I think she'd just have us all eating those prepackaged foods like she had when she was in the service. And while I think that we would be thankful for her cooking something, I'm not into rations."

"They're not all bad. I've eaten my fair share of them as well." He made a face that made her think he either didn't believe her or he'd had a couple of the more...well, tastier meals. "All right, I'll talk to Dustin and we'll go from there. Is it traditional foods? Or can you deviate from that a little?"

"I'd stick with traditional. I don't know why, but I'd think that Dad might be a little upset if there isn't any pumpkin pie and a turkey." She smiled at him. "I don't even want to know what you're thinking."

"What? I was just picturing of your dad's face if I were to put a tofu turkey in front of him, as well as braised carrots with a hint of dill." Parker shivered and she had to laugh. "I'll talk to Dustin, but expect the unexpected. Just putting that out there."

"You're going to be in so much trouble. Let me know when you're doing it. I want to have my camera pointed right at Dad when you do." He started for the door and turned back, this time looking serious. "I've not had a chance to tell you this, but welcome to the family. And thank you for making my brother very happy. You're a good egg, Mackenzie McCullough."

She sat there for several minutes after he left. There weren't a lot of things going on right now, so she leaned back and closed her eyes. Mackenzie knew that she was avoiding the envelope in front of her and what it meant to her. Staring at it wasn't going to make it disappear either. Instead of thinking about it anymore, she let her mind drift again.

Last night at dinner, Larson had told them about buying a new home. Rich and the others talked about all the things he was going to have to do to the house to get it livable, and he smiled and thanked them. Larson was so sweet, she wondered what sort of mate he'd have in his life. She hoped it was someone that would rock him out of his very straight life.

The babies were there too, a great distraction with all the manly talk going on. Mackenzie smiled when she thought of little Samuel in Dustin's arms, and the way he'd held him with such love and understanding. She wanted that for them too, soon. Purposely not thinking about the paperwork, she steered her mind to Thanksgiving.

She'd worked most of the holidays when she'd been in the service. There really was no other choice. Also, since being back in the States, she'd been more focused on keeping herself safe as well as taking care of her brother. Erwin was growing to love his new home, and she was going to have to make arrangements to have him home for dinner too.

She stared at the envelope. Then, sighing nervously, she picked it up and looked at it. It had arrived by courier this morning, and she'd only just now had the chance to look at what it was. Having a letter from the president was one thing, but to have a check the size it was made her think she was being punked.

Also, her student loans were now paid off, her insurance was paid up for the next fifty years, and she had a nice sized insurance policy in the event that something ever happened to her. Not likely, she knew, since she was as immortal as Jon. She wondered if Jarvis, as he insisted she call him, was aware of that.

Holding the check, she looked up and saw that at some point Dustin had joined her. Smiling at her, he took the check and letter from her and read it over before putting it back on her desk. Leaning back, she waited for him to comment.

"You do know that I can feel your emotions as well as you can, right?" Mackenzie shrugged. "I can. Also, when you are as distracted as you are, it does the same thing to me. I nearly cut my hand off twice when you drifted off. By the way, our new countertop has a small gouge in it. Nothing that can't be overlooked, but wanted you to know."

"I didn't expect it. This money, I mean. It's a great deal more than I think I would have made in the service." Dustin said he knew that, but it was nice. "Yes, it is. But too much. I mean, I'm sure that we can find a use for it somewhere, but it's a lot of unexpected money."

"I have an idea, if you want. No pressure." She asked him what it would be. "Put it in an account for college for our kids. I mean, when we have some, they'll need it, I think. And it can't hurt to have a little extra should they get a scholarship because they're so smart. You know, being our kids and all."

"You're goofy." He nodded and smiled at her. "Hawkins did this for me. He didn't have to, but it's very nice that he did. I was discharged without my benefits, so this will go a long way to our retirement years."

"You plan on retiring? I'm not. At least right now I'm not." She asked him what he wanted to do with their golden years. "What I'm doing now. Loving you. Keeping you beside me no matter what, and loving you."

"You said that twice. Not that I don't like it, but you did." He told her it bore repeating. "Oh Dustin, what did I ever do to deserve a wonderful man like you? And this family. They're all wonderful and kind. Nothing like I had growing up. You make a person feel welcome no matter how much they push you away."

"I'm the one that is blessed, baby. You've made me a complete man by being here with me." He stood up. "Now, how about you and I go and get us some lunch, maybe have some sex in the woods, and then you can get back to work. I know that I have a lot to do."

They did leave. Having lunch sounded wonderful, but the rest would have to wait, she told him. She had to meet with a patient at one, and then she had to go over some paperwork for Lauren for a case she was working on. The body, she'd told Mac, was all wrong for what she had read in the reports.

"She told me yesterday that she's been doing some things all wrong about death certificates. Instead of reading them for mistakes, she's been reading them for information. And autopsy reports too. Now that she's seen a couple that are filled out correctly, she is finding more and more things wrong." Dustin asked if she was going to work for Lauren. "No, not work, but I will help when she needs it. I can't imagine that would be too many times. She's pretty good at her job. And she's sort of scary too."

"She told me the same thing about you. You're scary smart, she said." Mackenzie just snorted at that. "You don't believe me? She said it in front of witnesses. I can call my dad if you want. We were all shocked by her admission. Even Mom."

"No, I mean that I'm not at all that smart. I'm just an average person who had to study hard to make it. I'm sure that a lot of you guys are much smarter." He just laughed and she wanted to smack him. "Seriously, I'm not all that brilliant."

"Really? How many heart and brain specialists do you know? I know one. I know a heart specialist, and I've heard of one brain surgeon, but never the same person doing both. You're very brilliant to me. And beautiful. That part you won't argue with me about. You're the most beautifully sexy woman I know."

They sat in the little café that had just opened a couple of weeks ago. The sun was shining brightly and there was a soft warm breeze that moved over them as they sat outside. It wouldn't last much longer, them being able to sit outside, so she enjoyed it while she could. When her tea was brought to her, she sipped it and looked around. This was such a wonderful little town, and she couldn't wait to bring up their children here. Looking at Dustin as he spoke to the couple next to them, she fell in love with him all over.

"I love you." He told her that he loved her as well. "I never thought I'd find someone to love again. I didn't even want to after Walton. I'm not comparing the two of you, but you're so different. Thank you, from the bottom of my heart, for being the one that my heart finally is open to."

He kissed her then, much to the amusement of those around them. Mackenzie could not wait for the rest of the women to come into this family. They were going to be loved like they'd never been before. And taken care of too. The McCulloughs were a breed apart from other men.

Chapter 14

Virginia finished up the book, and then sat back and let out a long breath. Her office was a complete disaster, and she had, more than likely, all her cups in this room and not a one in the kitchen. Picking up four that were still half full, she dumped the cold tea in the plant that looked as thirsty as she was. Making a mental note to water them, she went to the kitchen to find her mom doing dishes.

"How long have I been under?" Mom smiled at her. "That long, huh? Well, I have to work on getting the office back together, then I can start on the next one."

"No. We have a trip to make…that is, if you still want me to go with you." She'd hoped that she could get out of it, but told her mom that she did want her to go. "I'm going with you so you won't have to worry about things so much."

"I'm going to worry anyway." Mom nodded and told her to sit down. "I have two deadlines coming up. I have to go there and come back quickly. No playing around with lawyers who only want my money to pay off something Axel did."

"No, you don't have to worry about that either. I have it from your attorney that there is nothing you're going to be responsible for." Mom handed her a cup of tea, hot and fresh, just the way she normally took it. "And we both know that you're going to worry no matter how far you are from the deadlines. You're like that."

She was too. Sipping her tea, she thought of Axel. He'd been such a shit growing up. And most of the bad guys in her books were based on some of the things that he'd done to her and others. She had hated him since she was little, and it only got worse the older they got.

"Remember my ninth birthday party? The one that Axel came to with his parents?" Mom nodded and told her she was sorry again. "You wouldn't have known what he was going to do. I don't think any of us could have prepared for him coming there and making himself puke on my cake. But when he opened all my gifts, that was it for me. I washed my hands of him. I think even back then I knew that he'd be no good."

"Yes, and his father standing there with his camera laughing at him. I swear to you, that man should never have been able to breed. And his mother. My goodness, the way that she was dressed made me want to go and get the comforter off my bed and wrap her up in it." They both laughed. "He's gone now. I can't hardly believe that either. Never thought I'd say this about another human being, even one related to me, but the world more than likely made a sigh of relief when he passed on."

"But he killed Norine and left behind a little boy." Mom nodded and got up to make them some lunch. "What will become of him, you think? The little boy? He has no one to care for him. And as much as it pains me to say it, he'll be better off without his father there, teaching him how to be a bad person."

"There is that. I was thinking of all the things the little boy will be missing with both his parents gone. And I have to say, like you I think that he's going to be better off on his own. If he gets a family that isn't anything like his blood ones. I don't blame all of this on Axel. Norine should have known better when she married him, don't you think?" Virginia said she wasn't sure that the marriage was all that legal. "Well, whatever happened, it's over now. Except for Samuel."

"He'll be better off anywhere than with me, I'm thinking. I told that man that I spoke to that I don't know children. But the truth of the matter is, I'm afraid of them. They're... well, they're little people, and I don't care for people at all." Her mom said nothing, but continued to make them both a sandwich. "Mom, you agree with me, don't you?"

"Not necessarily. Yes, you do get lost in time when you work, but I'm here so that wouldn't be a problem. I do keep you from hurting yourself by forgetting to eat and shower and things." Virginia didn't agree or disagree with her mom. She had been here when she needed her, but a baby would mean so much more. "And it is your relative. Even though you hated Axel, justifiably so, the baby has nothing to do with who fathered him."

"I don't want my life messed up." Mom told her she was sure that Norine hadn't either. "Look. I'm going to go out there, settle up on whatever needs to be done, then come home. With you, to this house. No babies. No crap like bags full of baby crap or bottles. Nothing. All right?"

"Of course. You know what's best." Virginia growled at her mom, which caused her to laugh. "I'm sure you realize by now that you don't scare me like you do other people. How many cooks have you gone through this year alone? And I don't even want to think about housekeepers. My goodness, it's like a revolving door around here."

"I like my peace." Mom pointed out that vacuuming was a necessary evil. "Do they have to do it every day?"

"Yes, they should, and you should want them to. There is no telling what sort of creatures I might find in your carpet this time. How long as it been?" She told her. "Virginia, I've known of science projects that take less time than that. Six weeks is too long to go between cleanups. Why, if I didn't go in that office and gather mugs occasionally, we'd have our own batch of penicillin by now."

"It's not that bad." She'd not even noticed that her mom had been doing that. "What did I do around here before you came to stay with me?"

"I'm sure I don't want to know. By the way, I'm to tell you that your book signing has been set up in Europe for February of next year. And your agent called three days ago. Something about a model that wants to sit for you." Virginia dealt with the calls and then ate when her mom sat with her. "Virginia, when you go there, if you are keen on not bringing that child back with you, then I would suggest that you avoid seeing him at all costs. There is nothing that pulls at your heart strings like a small child."

"Some would say that I don't have a heart." Her mother told her to distance herself from those people. "I don't know. They might be right. I haven't had a date in...Christ, I don't know, at least since college. I don't do well with people. I hate going to the store for things because I hate crowds."

"I know you hate crowds, but there is hope for you." She

asked her how. "I'm not sure, but I'm thinking that it's out there. Eat your lunch, Virginia. We have a mess to tackle."

It took them both four hours to get her office back to rights. And then another two to take all the empty dishes to the kitchen and loaded in the dishwasher. Laundry was also done, things she wore to write then discarded as the day grew warmer or colder. Virginia sent her book to the editor and got out her notes on the next book. Tomorrow she would start fresh, as she did after each book she wrote.

Her cell was ringing as she made her way to the living room. Unknown wasn't a call that she ever took, and she let it go to voicemail. By the time she was settled in front of the television to watch it with Mom, there were four more calls, as well as messages from each one. She asked her mom what she should do.

"Why are you asking me such a thing? Answer it or listen to the messages. It might just be a sales call or something." Her mom stuck her tongue out at her, surprising her by the move. "Sometimes you act like such a child."

"Mom, you just stuck your tongue out at me. I think that alone would qualify you as a child." They were both laughing when she brought up the messages. "If this is an emergency, I'm going to be so pissed off." She put the phone on speaker so her mom could listen too.

"Miss Jacobson, my name is Joe Windfall. I'm the police officer that is handling your cousin's death, and that of his wife. If you could give me a call, I'd appreciate it. Nothing bad, I assure you, but I have one or two questions for you." He gave his number, then laughed. "By the way, if you don't call me back, I'm going to keep leaving messages."

"What an impertinent man." She had to agree with her

mom on that. "Call him back, answer his questions, then give him a piece of your mind. Or I will. It might be fun to use a few of those curse words that I read in your books."

"You read my books?" Mom nodded and laughed. "Don't. I swear if you quote them to me, I'm going to lose my shit. And I'll take care of him. And even if you haven't read them, don't start. That is something that will give me nightmares for the rest of my life."

"You're no fun, have I told you that lately? Anyway, my favorite line you've written so far is, 'get to it, chip dip.' I have no idea why I find that to be so funny." Neither did she. "Oh, and I wrote the number down for you. Just in case you deleted it before I could call him. Do you suppose he's cute? He sounds cute, doesn't he? I wonder if he has a big dick. All your men do, it seems. Your father had average, I guess you could call it in your books. Or a pencil one. I had to think on that for a while."

"Mom, you are forbidden to read my books again. And you're especially not allowed to talk to me about them." She just laughed and said she was going for more drinks. Virginia dialed the number and mumbled to herself about her mother. "I'm going to have her committed. Or put in a nursing home. I wonder if she'll read my books out loud to the others. Christ, that'd be so embarrassing when I went to see her."

"My mom said that most of the people in the home where she hangs out are more sexually active than she was as a newly married bride." Virginia started to end the call when Officer Windfall laughed. "Don't hang up, Miss Jacobson. I really do need to ask you a couple of things."

"You shouldn't comment on other people's embarrassing moments, sir." He said he was sorry. "I don't think you are.

196

There is a touch of humor in your voice that belies your comment. What is it you want to know?"

"First of all, let me tell you one thing. Your cousin had a long line of people that are going to be expecting someone to pay up. I want you to direct any and all calls you get to me. I'll make sure they don't bother you." She asked if they were dangerous. "A few might be. That's why I'm telling you to send them my way. I don't know if that'll work, but we have kept your name and relationship out of the papers here. And when you come to town, you can just use your pen name. I don't think that'll get you into trouble."

"You know I have a pen name?" He said that he had a friend who could find out about anything she set her mind to. "I see. Is this legal? I mean, what would she need to do that for?"

"To make sure that when you come to town, you're nothing like your cousin was." Virginia didn't comment. "Miss Jacobson, the couple of things I'd like to know are, did you know if Axel was involved with anyone? Not like a girlfriend or his wife, but others. The unsavory type."

"No. I mean, I knew that he was trouble…he has been since we were kids. And if he was, it wouldn't surprise me one bit. He did some prison time when he was younger. Even juvie house before that. His parents are gone, thankfully, because they didn't help him one bit when he got into trouble. And Axel was forever in trouble with something." He thanked her for her honesty. "I know that he did some jail time for beating a man over a pool game, but I don't know all of that. Not prison, but then I didn't keep up with him."

"He did a five year stretch in the state pen here, plus, he had a trial coming up that would have put him away for more. Too bad that it wasn't sooner rather than later. Norine, his wife, she seemed to have her stuff together until she met him. We're trying to piece that relationship together now." Virginia told him that she had only seen the woman a couple of times. "She didn't know that her brother is gone. I'm not sure why she wasn't notified, but as I said, we're looking into all matter of things here."

"She told me once that he knocked her up, and she wasn't sure that they were married legally. But she lost the baby not long later. I think she fell or something. At least that's what she told me. I don't believe that now or then. Like I said, Axel wasn't a good person." Joe told her that they were married, as far as he could find. "This baby, is he all right? I mean, I know that he knocked her around quite a bit."

"He's going to be fine. The hospital here has given him a clean bill of health. And he's with very good people." She asked if they were going to adopt him. "Doubtful. Mr. and Mrs. McCullough have six boys that are grown up and some married. The youngest is in his late twenties, I think."

"Wow, that poor woman." She laughed when he did, not sure what he found to be funny. "I'm leaving in two days. My mom and I will be flying out. Like I said before to the doctor, I can't stay long. I have a deadline to keep. Any other questions for me?"

"Yes, ma'am. My wife, she'd like to know if you'd sign a couple of her books. She's promised not to tell anyone that you're coming, but she really would be happy if you'd do that for her. She doesn't get out much, what with her being in a chair and all. If you don't have time—"

"No, I'd love to do that for her. Tell her that I appreciate her keeping it quiet, but that I'd be honored to sign whatever books she has." He told her that on a cop's salary, she didn't have many but she would love that. "Good. All right then, if there is nothing else, I'll see you in a few days."

"All right then. Thank you very much. And like I said, you just tell them, if they call, that they should call me." Virginia assured him that she would. "Safe travels."

When her mom returned, she told her what was going on. She also told her about the books she was going to sign. Mom told her about the shipment that had come in a few days ago, and that she could take her that book.

"That's a wonderful idea. I'm sure that I can look around here and find a few more too. I love it." The movie was forgotten as they made a search of the office, which was much easier since it was cleaned up. "I'll have to send her more too. I have no idea, but I think I might like her. Her husband is a nice guy."

For the first time since she'd gotten the call, she was feeling excited. Virginia hated to travel. Actually, she hated leaving home at all. But this trip, it might be what she needed. And she'd get some more characters' traits for future stories. Lord knew her mom gave her enough.

~~~

Mackenzie was making rounds when she heard Erwin shouting her name. She knew that he was coming around today—they were going to have lunch—but she hadn't expected him to be so loud. Finding him with Dustin was a nice treat too.

"You have to keep your voice down, buddy. There are people resting here." Erwin told him he'd try, but he was so excited. "Yeah, me too. But I don't want us to get kicked out, do you?"

"No sir, I surely don't." He'd been hanging around with Rich, and it was showing in his language. "Do you suppose we can go fishing again? Grandpa said that he'd take me again, but he has to have help. I'm too... I can't remember what he called me. He said it wasn't a bad thing."

"Too energetic. And he's right about that." She heard Erwin's laughter and then Dustin's. "There she is. Be careful now."

Erwin ran to her, but he was careful to stop running before he got all the way to her. His hugs could be too strong at times, but he was gentle with her today. Mackenzie told him he'd done a good job. "You two going to join me for lunch? My goodness, what's a girl to do with two handsome men to eat with?" Erwin giggled again and held her hand. "What have you been up to? I heard you went fishing."

As he went on about his time on the water, she watched him. To see him so happy was something that she wasn't used to. He still had some bad days where he'd be upset for no apparent reason, but those were few and far between now. They went to the cafeteria in the lower levels, and she watched him pick out his meal. Dustin kissed her neck when she was seated with them.

Dustin told her about Larson's house and what they were working on now. She told him about her day so far. Erwin just enjoyed his meal. When he was finished, he asked if he could have his tablet and Dustin handed it to him.

"I told him no electronics at the table while eating. They must do that at the home he's at too." She said that it was a rule. "I've got some news about our house too. It'll be done next week. Like completely done. I cannot wait. This is why I like working on empty homes instead of ones with people in them. Less rules."

Her beeper went off about the time her name was being called over the PA system. Standing up, she told them that she'd see them both later and headed to the ER. Doctoring was always a crapshoot about getting to finish a meal, but she loved her job and wouldn't trade it for the world now.

Before You Go...

HELP AN AUTHOR

write a review

THANK YOU!

Share your voice and help guide other readers to these wonderful books. Even if it's only a line or two your reviews help readers discover the author's books so they can continue creating stories that you'll love. Login to your favorite retailer and leave a review. Thank you.

AWARD WINNING, BESTSELLING AUTHOR

Kathi Barton, winner of the Pinnacle Book Achievement award as well as a best-selling author on Amazon and All Romance books, lives in Nashport, Ohio with her husband Paul. When not creating new worlds and romance, Kathi and her husband enjoy camping and going to auctions. She can also be seen at county fairs with her husband who is an artist and potter.

Her muse, a cross between Jimmy Stewart and Hugh Jackman, brings her stories to life for her readers in a way that has them coming back time and again for more. Her favorite genre is paranormal romance with a great deal of spice. You can visit Kathi online and drop her an email if you'd like. She loves hearing from her fans. aaronskiss@gmail.com.

Follow Kathi on her blog: http://kathisbartonauthor. blogspot.com/

www.ingramcontent.com/pod-product-compliance
Lightning Source LLC
Chambersburg PA
CBHW032128170626
46808CB00006B/2152